3

"Stamp your blood print here... Hmm, ten years is a really long time, isn't it? Surely there's a way we can speed things along?"

GRIMM

An archbishop with a lot of baggage.

■ **AGENT SIX'S VIEW**

The marriage contract is nothing to sneeze at, but the implied threat of curses for a broken promise is an even bigger pain in the ass! This is exactly what I'm talking about when I say she's got a lot of baggage!

THIS VOLUME'S MAIN HEROINE

ROSE'S VIEW
I'd appreciate it if you'd stop treating me like we're related, Mr. Russell. Some of us actually take life seriously, you know...

"Tiger Man, there's something wrong with me. I feel strange. My heart won't stop racing..."

THE UNDEAD FESTIVAL: FUN FOR GUYS, GIRLS, AND EVERYONE IN BETWEEN!

RUSSELL

A Chimera known as Russell of the Water. Idol and mother figure to the Combat Agents.

"You've always been strrrange, but there's nothing wrong nyeow. What's cute is cute. Just accept it."

"Welcome! I'm this club's number one hostess, Snow."

SNOW

A diligent woman who rose from the slums to become the number one hostess at an overpriced hostess club. She's steadily losing sight of what she ought to value as a knight.

THE UNDEAD FESTIVAL: FUN FOR UNSAVORY TYPES, TOO!

"Hey, you there! We've got boobies here! Big boobies! Whaddaya think? We're doin' a four-for-one boob deal if you act now!"

This is the city's hospitality district. Using money borrowed from Alice, we've rented a small space for the festival.

"C'mon, bro, you know what I'm talkin' about! Boobies, of course! They're soft, warm, and make you happy just by lookin' at 'em! Everyone loves boobies!"

"Everyone loves…"

"Boobies, yes."

There aren't any hostess clubs in this town. There are more direct forms of prostitution like brothels, but perhaps there just isn't much demand for bars where men can drink surrounded by beautiful women. After all, this country has way more women than men.

I smile at the customer, rubbing my hands together.

"For just five silver pieces an hour, you can spend time with some pretty young women. How about it? Refresh yourself with tasty booze and bountiful boobies."

"I'm in."

Seems this guy doesn't have much resistance to this sort of thing, as he accepts the invitation quite readily.

I show him inside before he changes his mind.

■ALICE'S VIEW
What do you mean you only see two boobs, huh? You trying to start a fight? This is the optimal size for high-spec functionality! Got it?

<I'm fueled by a great sense of rage. I won't be so easily cleansed.>

GIANT STUFFED CAT
....
?????

AN INCIDENT AT THE UNDEAD FESTIVAL

"Undeath is Lord Zenarith's specialty. There's only one thing to do here!"

CONTENTS

Prologue
P. 001

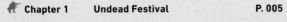
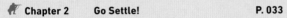

Epilogue
P. 165

COMBATANTS WILL BE DISPATCHED!

COMBATANTS WILL BE DISPATCHED!

3

Natsume Akatsuki

ILLUSTRATION BY
Kakao Lanthanum

YEN ON
NEW YORK

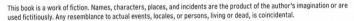

COMBATANTS WILL BE DISPATCHED!

Natsume Akatsuki 3

Translation by Noboru Akimoto
Cover art by Kakao Lanthanum

SENTOIN, HAKEN SHIMASU! Volume 3
© Natsume Akatsuki, Kakao • Lanthanum 2019
First published in Japan in 2019 by KADOKAWA CORPORATION, Tokyo.
English translation rights arranged with KADOKAWA CORPORATION, Tokyo through
TUTTLE-MORI AGENCY, INC., Tokyo.

English translation © 2020 by Yen Press, LLC

Yen On
150 West 30th Street, 19th Floor
New York, NY 10001

Visit us at yenpress.com
facebook.com/yenpress
twitter.com/yenpress
yenpress.tumblr.com
instagram.com/yenpress

First Yen On Edition: April 2020

Yen On is an imprint of Yen Press, LLC.
The Yen On name and logo are trademarks of Yen Press, LLC.

The publisher is not responsible for websites (or their content) that are not owned by the publisher.

Library of Congress Cataloging-in-Publication Data
Names: Akatsuki, Natsume, author. | Lanthanum, Kakao, illustrator. | Akimoto, Noboru, translator.
Title: Combatants will be dispatched! / Natsume Akatsuki ; illustration by Kakao Lanthanum ; translation by
    Noboru Akimoto ; cover art by Kakao Lanthanum.
Other titles: Sentoin haken shimasu!. English
Description: First Yen On edition. | New York : Yen On, 2019.
Identifiers: LCCN 2019025056 | ISBN 9781975385583 (v. 1 ; trade paperback) |
    ISBN 9781975331528 (v. 2 ; trade paperback) | ISBN 9781975399023 (v. 3 ; trade paperback)
Subjects: CYAC: Science fiction. | Robots—Fiction.
Classification: LCC PZ7.1.A38 Se 2019 | DDC [Fic]—dc23
LC record available at https://lccn.loc.gov/2019025056

ISBNs: 978-1-9753-9902-3 (paperback)
978-1-9753-0863-6 (ebook)

10 9 8 7 6 5 4 3 2 1

LSC-C

Printed in the United States of America

"That about covers it, Six. You still with me?"

"No, not at all."

This particular night, I'm being given a nonsensical briefing over the monitor.

Lilith the Black is on the other end. She lets out an exasperated sigh at my failure.

"Six, you may be a meathead, but I thought you were at least as smart as an elementary schooler. I'll explain one more time."

The self-proclaimed genius tomboy shakes her head.

"Agent Six, you're currently on probation. The forced requisitioning of the Destroyer has caused your Evil Points to fall deep into the red. As a result, we're limiting your access to the requisition system."

"That's what I don't get. I'm here putting my life on the line to beat back our competition. The Destroyer's just part of the cost of doing business. In fact, you should be giving me a bonus for all my hard work."

The Kisaragi Corporation's pride and joy, the multilegged combat vehicle we called the Destroyer, is an assault weapon developed by the woman on the screen in front of me.

We forced them to send us one so we could defeat another of the Demon Lord's Elite Four...

"We've got our hands full here on Earth. We need every fighter we can get our hands on, even lowly minions like you. Yet, you ordered one of our top-class weapons, then let the competition damage it, to boot...!"

"It's not like we had much choice. According to Alice, they had the higher-spec machine. The Destroyer took damage because its inventor is useless."

"U-u-u-useless? You're calling *me* useless?!"

Lilith seems particularly sensitive to the slight. I suppose it's because everyone around her is quick to praise her genius on a day-to-day basis.

"If anything, you should be praising us for sending their higher-spec machine to the scrapyard. But that's fine for now. The real problem is with these new orders."

"It's not fine, but we'll table that discussion. As for your new orders...you're referring to the orders to build a hideout, right?"

Kisaragi's newly issued orders.

They want us to build an entire fortress to serve as our base of operations on this planet.

"Last time you had us secure territory, and now you want us to build a base? You're working us a little too hard. With this latest restriction of yours, I can't even spend Evil Points! How are we supposed to build a base with no equipment?"

"We'll let you order the equipment you need to build the base. But no more negative point totals, all right? If you need supplies, put some effort into your villainy."

Ah, so they'll send me stuff that's not weaponry—good to know.

I'll insist that things like porn and recreational items are necessary for base construction and have them send some over.

"Your thought process is easy enough to read. I'll make sure they don't send you anything like adult books or comics."

"You sure you wanna cut us off from all relaxation? We might take advantage of our new base and rebel."

"If that happens, we'll send Astaroth over to put you in your place. She's been on edge lately as it is."

Lilith seems amused by Astaroth's current state.

"What's wrong with Astaroth? She on the rag? Go ahead and send her some pads as a present from me. Then tell her to treat us a little better and stop giving us these awful assignments."

"Y-you really are a piece of shit. Astaroth's on edge because she hasn't seen a *certain someone* lately... Oh well. Agent Six, you've currently got an Evil Point deficit. Ordinarily, that would mean the punishment unit would come after you, but I've taken measures to delay that. Temporarily. Take the time to do some real villainy and get your points back up."

Lilith lets out a playful little chuckle.

"Let's just say you owe me one."

She then reaches over to cut the connection...

"Ahem. You know you still owe *me*, right? I haven't forgotten about the fact that you zapped me over here without explaining a god-damn thing. When I get back, I'm gonna grope you till you cry."

"......What?"

"I'm gonna grope you till you cry."

"Well then, Agent Six! We'll leave the base construction to you! Until we meet again..."

"I'm gonna grope you till you cr—"

"I'm sorry! I really am! I'll give you a proper apology eventually, so please forgive me!"

1

Kisaragi Corporation Grace Kingdom branch.

"Tiger Man, there's something wrong with me. I feel strange. My heart won't stop racing..."

"You've always been strrrange, but there's nothing wrong nyeow. What's cute is cute. Just accept it."

Here in a suburban house currently given the ridiculously exaggerated role of a hideout, Tiger Man and I sit discussing the deep truths of the world.

"But—but...this is a guy! Why am I getting so worked up?"

"It's not like I preferrrr guys, either. It's just that genderrrr doesn't matter to me if they're cute."

"It sure matters to me!"

While we're having this conversation, Russell is busily cleaning the windows in the French maid costume he's been forced to wear, staring daggers at us the whole time.

*　　*　　*

It hasn't been that long since we got into a war with the neighboring kingdom of Toris over an unfortunate misunderstanding. During that conflict, we managed to capture Russell of the Water.

Despite his initial resistance, Russell has submitted to his role, making good use of his abilities to create water for the kingdom.

And now...

...due to Tiger Man's wishes, he's somehow ended up working as a maid for Kisaragi.

Tiger Man and I crouch down, gazing up Russell's skirt from below.

"What do you think, Tiger Man? I still think black panties and maid outfits don't mix."

"You rrreally don't get it, do you? Maids are right next to nuns on the hotness scale. The gap between purrception and rrreality; the whole sense of taboo. That's what makes maids with black underwear so grrrrreat!"

Yeah, I don't get it.

"Tiger Man, are you using big words to sound smarter? I still don't get what you're saying, so I'd appreciate it if you could put it a little more simply."

"I was trrrrying to explain it in a way that even a complete idiot would underrrstand... *Sigh.* Let me trrry it this way. I'll use Agent Eight as an example. She's constantly in and out of pet shops when she's off duty. She'd love to own a pet, but she's afrrrraid she'd fall aparrrt if it died."

Agent Eight, unlike me, is an actual elite agent. She even has the latest body enhancements.

She's ridiculously beautiful and has a figure to die for, but she's a bit of a loner, which makes it hard to get to know her.

"You serious? All this time, she's been pushing the cool beauty persona even though she has a cutesy side? I'm definitely gonna tease her about it next time I see her."

"Let me know when you do. She's too big for my tastes, but I loooove watching an emotionally detached beauty turn beet red from embarrassment. Anyway, that's a great example of the gap between purrrception and rrreality."

Ah, I sorta get it now.

The two of us grab at the unresponsive Russell's skirt hem, staring intently upward.

"When you put it like that, I can see how black panties for maids could work."

"I know, right? There arrre some who say maids should only wear white panties, but I'm a black-pantie Tiger Man through and through."

Just as we appear to have come to an understanding, the room's door opens.

"Boss. Grimm's calling. She says it's an emergency and needs you at the castle ASAP..."

Rose appears in the doorway.

As I wonder what the hell Grimm might want, Rose catches the two of us peeking up Russell's skirt and freezes.

I keep hold of the skirt hem, lifting it slightly as I respond.

"What does she want now? Bother me later; I'm busy."

"Are you *that* busy peeking up Russell's skirt?! No, that's not the problem! Wait...! What are you doing, Boss? And you, too, Tiger Man! I mean, Russell's a guy, so why are you even in this situation to begin with?"

As Rose babbles in confusion, Russell, who had been quietly cleaning the windows, lets out a deep sigh.

"...I'm not dressed this way by choice, you know. Tiger Man said he'd release me early if I did my work while wearing this outfit... Hey, you're a Battle Chimera like me, right? Humans really are fools, aren't they? Especially the ones here...," Russell says sagely.

"You say that now, Rrrussell, but when I use you as a body pillow everrry night, you don't seem to mind. Even if you do complain about my furrr!"

"...Whatever! H-hey, Rose, don't look at me like that! It's not what you think! It's just cuddling! We haven't done anything more than that! We haven't crossed that line!"

As Rose eyes him with disgust, Russell begins rattling off excuses.

"You're quite the gentleman, Tiger Man. I figured you'd have already devoured him by now."

"I don't like making little kids crrry. I'm patiently waiting for Rrrussell to come around."

Russell heaves a weary sigh and shakes his head slowly. "That'll never happen. Just give it up... C-come on now, don't look at me like that, Rose! We're kin! I'm not doing this because I want to! I'm hurt... Uh, anyway, wasn't there something you were here to do?"

At that, Rose snaps back to reality. "Th-that's right! This isn't the time to be panicking over Mr. Russell's fetishes."

"W-wait, Sister, what do you mean 'fetishes'?!"

Putting aside Russell's tearful objection, Rose looks at me with a serious expression.

"Grimm wants you to bring her some dolls."

"......"

I resume peering up Russell's skirt.

2

"Boss, are you sure you actually like women? Are you sure you don't have weird fetishes like Mr. Russell?"

"Lay off already. I was just momentarily confused. If you keep doubting me, I can use your body to prove just how much I love women."

We're on the way to the castle, and Rose is still peering at me suspiciously. I drop into a fighting stance to make my point.

"I—I got it. I believe you! I believe you, so please stop with those gestures!" Rose backs off cautiously as I approach with my wriggling fingers at the ready.

Coming out of my stance, I ask a question that pops into my head. "Hey, I heard you haven't asked Russell about your identity. Why not? You've been looking for those answers for ages, haven't you?"

Rose's brow twitches...

"Well... Now that it's staring me in the face, I'm a little afraid to know the truth... Mr. Russell really hates humans. I'm scared that I won't be able to keep living this way if I know my identity." She looks down with an expression of unease...

"Hey, look at that stall! Mokemokes! They're selling mokemoke skewers!"

"Please don't change the subject! I'm trying to be serious right now! And you were the one who started this, Boss!"

God, she's needy.

"I've been addicted to mokemokes lately. They might look like giant crawfish, but they're delicious. And it turns out they're a delicacy!"

"Boss, weren't you calling mokemokes your friends not that long ago? What's changed?" Rose asks. I have no idea what she's talking about.

"Why would I be friends with crawfish? You really do say some weird things from time to time. Hey, can I get two mokemoke skewers? One sauced, the other salted."

"That's my line! Did you already forget?! You did, didn't you?! Boss, what's wrong with your memory?!"

She can't seem to drop this utterly irrelevant topic, so I hold out the two skewers I just bought.

"Sauced or salted?"

"Sauced, please... But don't think you're pulling one over on me! I'm not that easy! Not with just one mokemoke skewer..."

Two hours later, we arrive at the castle's training grounds, where we're accosted by Grimm. Apparently, she's been waiting here the whole time.

"You're late! I told you to hurry because it's an emergency! Where are the dolls? You *did* buy some dolls, right?!"

As part of some shady ritual, Grimm is frantically attaching little labels to a bunch of human-shaped mud clumps sliding around the training grounds.

Wait—wait, what...?

"Wh-what the hell are those wiggly things...?"

"They're evil spirits! I can't just let them roam free, so I've trapped them inside mud figurines! But never mind that, Commander, where are the dolls?!"

At Grimm's unusually urgent pleading, I reach into my jacket and take *it* out...

"Here's Meat the Ripper, the Kisaragi Corporation's mascot. He talks if you press the button on his back."

"HI, I'M MEAT! TIME TO SLAUGHTER HEROES!"

"Ugh! What is this creepy thing?! It doesn't have a shred of cuteness! I wanted you to bring me stuffed animals! We cram evil spirits into cute things so that we *won't* be creeped out when they come to life!"

Still, looking at the mud lumps wiggling around at my feet, I feel like putting these into stuffed animals would just double their creepiness.

"Boss, if Grimm doesn't want it, I'll take Meat. He's pretty cute."

"Seriously? There's something majorly wrong with your tastes, Rose! ...Say, Rose, you've got sauce around your mouth. What were you doing?"

Taking Meat from me, Rose holds him up to hide her mouth.

"HI! I'M MEAT! TIME TO SLAUGHTER SPINSTERS!"

"Rose, give me that doll! It's clearly evil! Why did you press the button anyway?!"

Just then...

...as Grimm tries to grab Meat, the mud dolls at her feet start shaking uncontrollably.

"Hey. There seems to be something wrong with these..."

"Huh? ...Eeep! Oh no!" Grimm says hurriedly before scurrying behind my back.

At the same time, the mud dolls explode with a dry *pop*, and mud splashes across my face and Rose's.

"...Rose, hold Grimm down."

"HI! I'M MEAT! TIME TO SLAUGHTER INCOMPETENT LACKEYS!"

"Commander? Just listen, please...? Rose, calm down... Two on one isn't fair!" Grimm looks at us fearfully as we inch closer. "The Undead Festival's about to start! It'll be a disaster without me! Commander, I'm so sorry! Please, please waaaaiiit!"

<Evil Points Acquired>

"Oh, right. You did mention something about an undead festival, didn't you?"

Punishing Grimm a little has helped me calm down, and I listen to Rose's explanation as Grimm softly sobs next to us.

Magic is commonplace on this planet, and so are undead, apparently.

"The Undead Festival is a ritual where you welcome back the spirits of our dead ancestors. It takes place around this time each year. I like it because it means you get to eat lots of delicious food for free."

"Ah, so it's a bit like Obon back home."

However, unlike Obon in Japan, here the ancestral spirits literally come home. And it seems that these spirits, unless provided mediums to possess, end up possessing random corpses and wandering around town.

"*Sob*... Wh-which is why, as the Archbishop of Lord Zenarith, God of Undeath and Disaster, I am in charge of organizing the festivities... The reason those mud dolls blew up was because they were temporary mediums. They couldn't hold up under the strain."

"...Ah well, I think I get the gist of it. So what happened to the evil spirits, then? Can I go home now?"

Grimm looks at me with a grave expression, shaking her head slowly. "There's only a week until the Undead Festival. I need to prepare enough vessels for the ancestors to possess. Commander, I'd like your help in gathering materials to make the dolls."

"Sounds like a pain in the ass, so I'm gonna have to say no. Rose, I'm sure you're still hungry. Let's grab something on the way home. Any requests?"

"HI! I'M MEAT! COMBAT AGENTS SHOULD EAT MEAT!"

"Pleeeease! If you'll help me, I'll make it worth your while! I'll give you all sorts of sexual favors!"

As I turn to leave, Grimm clings to my hips, crying as she begs for help.

"Sexual favors? I already sexually harass you as a way of saying hello..."

"That's true! You hiked up my skirt and did all sorts of things to me before! If you're not going to help me out now, then you should take responsibility for earlier and support me!"

And now she's turning this back on *me*.

"All right, fine. I'll hold you to those favors. But keep in mind that we're both grown adults. If you try to pass off a kiss as a reward like Snow did, nudity is going to be the least of your worries."

"...Actually, Commander, do you mind if I have a little longer to think it over?"

3

Returning to the hideout, I let Alice know I'll be helping with the Undead Festival.

"So I'll be helping out with this weird festival."

"...I really want to disrupt that festival. Seriously? Undead? Feels like they're challenging me as an android." Alice reacts rather poorly to the mention of the undead. As a product of modern science, she just can't stand illogical and superstitious things. "Hey, Six, you're already a gullible meathead. Don't fall for Grimm's scams."

"From my end, I have to wonder why you're so skeptical of supernatural events."

Putting aside Alice's (admittedly typical) foul mood, I decide then to ask the question that's been nagging at me since I got here.

"...What's *she* doing here?"

Alice is seated in a chair, and next to her, Snow is hunched over, working intently on something while beads of sweat form on her brow.

"Looks like she's finally flat broke thanks to the loans she took out to pay for her magic swords. I saw her seriously contemplating whether or not to sell her body, so I decided to shoulder her debt and have her make ammo for me in return."

"I don't even know where to start."

Maybe with the fact that this unicorn-pure knight was about to sell her body?

Or the fact that she owes Alice—a child by all appearances—a lot of money?

Or how about the fact that a ballistics amateur is currently fiddling with gunpowder?

"Alice, I'm done! I finished another round."

"I thought I told you to call me Miss Alice while you still owe me money?"

"I'm done, Miss Alice."

"Good. Still room for improvement, but you're getting better at this."

Snow smiles happily, her fingertips stained black with gunpowder. Alice's praise for her handiwork seems to have really made Snow's day.

It's hard to believe she was the knight captain of the Royal Guard until recently. Now she's fallen so low that she's showing deference to a child and forcibly making shotgun shells for said child.

"You know... She's still part of my squadron. Seeing her like this kind of hurts..."

Snow doesn't so much as glance in my direction, finishing up the next round and retrieving it from the equipment. "Miss Alice! I finished another one! I'm pretty proud of it!"

"Hey, not bad at all! If you can keep up this quality and speed up the process, your hourly rate might get a boost."

"Yay!"

My eyes sting as I watch Snow's happy reaction.

"...? What's your problem, Six? Stop staring at me with those lecherous eyes of yours. If you lay a finger on me, you'll have to pay up."

...I can't say I feel much sympathy for her.

4

That evening...

"Are you ready, Commander? Come on, Rose. Push me more carefully!"

A tightly wound Grimm has summoned Rose and me again.

"...So we're going to gather materials for your dolls, right?"

"That's right... Come on, Rose, faster! We'll ride the wind!"

"It's too risky! If we go too fast, you'll fall off, Grimm! Besides, I just had a big dinner, and now I'm getting sleepy...," Rose complains drearily.

"And that's why you're still a child! The night is young! Come on, I'll show you how grown-ups like me have fun after dark!" Grimm declares as her wheelchair is slowly pushed along.

"Uh, not that I have anything against enjoying the nightlife, but do we really have to leave the city? I thought we were here to gather materials."

"That's right. I keep telling you, we're going to gather materials for the dolls."

....

"What exactly do you use for these?"

"Plants from the Cursed Forest."

Rose and I turn around.

"Hey, wait! Do you know what'll happen if a frail maiden like me goes into the Cursed Forest alone? There are barbarians in that forest! If they see a tasty morsel like me, they won't be able to resist their carnal desires! Are you okay with your precious subordinate becoming damaged goods, Commander?"

"And you wonder why no one's interested in you. Go hook one of those barbarians and settle down already. A spinster with unrealistic marriage expectations is too much of a ticking time bomb for anyone else."

Grimm scowls at my response. "That's going too far, even for you, Commander! I've got plenty of interested suitors! I'm the Archbishop of Zenarith! Got it? A priestess has to remain pure of body for..."

"Hey, there's something hopping around over there. Rose, go catch one. See how it tastes."

"That's a mipyokopyoko. They explode in your mouth if you try to eat them."

"Listen to meeeeee!"

Grimm throws a tantrum in her wheelchair. We're already out of town; I wish she'd quiet down.

"I'm impressed you noticed it in this darkness, Boss."

"My body mods include basic night vision. You're pretty impressive yourself. All I saw was a weird shape hopping around in the distance."

Grimm starts smacking me on the back. Begging for attention, I guess. "Commander, I can see in the dark, too! As the God of Undeath, Lord Zenarith rules the night, after all, and provides appropriate blessings to his archbishop!"

"That's nice."

"Why are you always so cold to me? If you keep that up, I'll curse you!"

Suddenly, off in the distance, another indistinct figure leaps into the air.

"I just saw something else hopping around. Is that a mipyo-kopyoko, too?"

"That's a mupyokopyoko! Let's catch and boil it!"

"Enough with the pyoko-pyoko-pyoko-pyokoing! Both of you, listen to me!" Grimm tearfully pleads, holding on to Rose before she can go off hunting.

"Let's just catch it and go home. We can make hot pot at the hideout. Besides, it's getting late anyway."

"The fact that it's nighttime is the whole point! I need a flower that only blooms under moonlight! The flower acts as a permission slip for dead spirits to stay in the world. It's how we keep the spirits from turning evil!" Grimm vehemently pleads her case as she latches onto Rose's tail. "Commander, please don't go home. The festival will be a disaster without enough possession dolls. It's a chance for you to make up for your usual crimes."

"...*Sigh*. If Grimm's this committed, I think we should help her. She's right about it being a good chance to reflect on your behavior, Boss." Rose seems to be at her limit.

"Can I point out that I wasn't born this way? My personality's the result of how my parents raised me. Kids don't get to pick their parents. It's not like I want to be this way," I inform them, and Rose and Grimm gasp.

"I-I'm so sorry, Boss. I guess you've had a rough life, too." Rose looks down, likely reminded of her own struggles with her grandfather's teachings.

"My parents used to tell me to actively do things people don't like. I'm just doing as I was taught."

"Apologize to your parents! You're totally misinterpreting what they told you!"

I half-heartedly dismiss Rose's lecture as Grimm takes something out.

It's a well-worn dagger that seems to have been handled with care, although I don't know who it belongs to.

I've never seen her use a weapon, so I'm assuming it's an object with some sentimental value that she plans to use for a curse.

"...So, Commander, do you remember how the prince of Toris became impotent due to the effects of my curse...?"

"Wait, Grimm. What are you talking about? What the hell did you do when we weren't looking?" I ask her.

Grimm smiles thinly as Rose grabs her by the shoulders and shakes her back and forth.

"I recommend you help me while I'm asking nicely. I can't promise things will stay that way otherwise..."

How impressively evil. I suppose that's to be expected from the follower of a dark god.

But she needs to choose her targets more carefully.

"Bold of you to threaten the agent of an evil organization. But my profession means I can't back down when threatened. I'll answer your threat with a threat of my own."

"Wait, Boss, what's this about an evil organization?! You never told me about that. That's the group you forcibly recruited me into, isn't it?!" Rose grabs and shakes me instead, but I push her aside and assume a fighting stance in front of Grimm.

"If you curse me, I'll sexually harass you until you beg for mercy and break the curse. It'll make the things I did to you while you were passed out in the desert look tame by comparison."

"Wait, Commander, what do you mean? Just what did you do to me in the desert while I was out cold? Tell me!"

5

The Cursed Forest near the kingdom of Grace—a land damned and abandoned by the locals, infested with monsters and mysterious tribes of barbarians.

We've arrived in the forest after a few arguments along the way. We're now looking for the flower in question.

"Hey, you two, that white flower's the one we're looking for. Frail old me will wait here while you go pick them." Grimm makes a ludicrous demand at the entrance to the forest.

"Yeah…no."

"It's not like I can do anything about it. I can't go in there with my wheelchair."

"That reminds me. You can walk just fine. You don't need that wheelchair. You can get by without shoes."

The backlash from a curse she cast a long time ago left her unable to wear shoes, which leaves me wondering why the hell she tried a curse like that to begin with.

"Wheelchairs are pretty convenient, you know. I don't have to expend any effort because other people push me around, and you'd think I was a frail, sickly beauty at first glance, right?"

"People with actual disabilities might have a problem with that, you know," I say with an exasperated sigh.

Rose tugs lightly at my sleeve.

"Boss, I think Grimm's fine the way she is. It's a hassle to move her around when she's sleeping during the day. Not to mention the fact that she dies the moment you take your eyes off her, so it's easier to carry her around with a wheelchair."

"You know, I've been meaning to talk about how you treat me while I'm dead..."

Rose and I wander around under the moonlight, picking the flowers Grimm wanted.

We're still at the entrance to the forest, but I hear random cries from time to time.

I can't wait to get out of here and grab a drink.

"Hey, Grimm, it doesn't have to be fancy, but make sure you take me to a place where I can drink with beautiful women, okay?"

"...? Huh? What are you talking about?"

"I'm okay with something cheap so long as I get to eat a lot."

"What are you two talking about?! Wait...am I supposed to take you two out after we're done here?! But this is work for the kingdom!"

At that moment, I hear something crawling toward us. It's probably reacting to Grimm's yelling.

Rose and Grimm fall quiet. They seem to have noticed the creatures moving to surround us.

"Why do you always make things so difficult? Oh well—don't worry about it. Kisaragi operatives don't abandon their comrades. Besides, cleaning up an incompetent lackey's mess is part of my job description."

"Now wait just a minute! Sure, it's probably my yelling that drew them over, but still!"

"I've gotten used to cleaning up after Grimm. Hey, Grimm, I'd like five extra-large servings of *yakiniku*."

"All right, all right! I'm sorry. Thanks for always protecting me and resurrecting me!"

I look at the sobbing Grimm out of the corner of my eye before staring into the darkness...

"Looks like six enemy humanoids. I'll take three; you two deal with the rest." I draw my knife from my back holster and brace myself.

Rose steps up next to me and cracks her knuckles. "Roger. I'll take two! You can count on me when it comes to fighting!"

It's times like this I'm glad to have a Battle Chimera at my side.

So that leaves one more...

"Wait, what?! I can't fight directly, so you shouldn't include me in your head count!"

......

"...Oh, for the love of—! Fine, whatever! I'll take four of them! Sheesh, Grimm, you're useless!"

"Please don't say that! You just need to remember my great powers have to be used at the right time and place! You can't waste curses on random minions..."

As Grimm starts to make her excuses, Rose, who had been twitching her nose, falls silent with a serious expression on her face.

Rose's change in attitude makes me distinctly uneasy, but I shine my light toward the hostile creatures.

Even though I can see in the dark, it's always better to fight with sufficient light.

I want to catch a glimpse of who is lurking around out here...

"Graaaaaahhh!"

"Aiiiiieeeeee!"

The light reveals a rotting corpse.

After letting out a threatening roar, the corpse reacts to my scream by shambling toward me.

"A z-zombie?! That's a zombie, right? America's favorite monster?!"

I mean, I guess it's not surprising there's zombies in a world with demons and ghosts.

It's not surprising, but…

"I don't know what America is, but please calm down, Boss."

"I don't care how strong they are! It's how they look that's a problem! Gotta calm down. I'm an elite Kisaragi operative. I-I'm not a-afraid. Sorry, corpse, but I'm gonna cremate you with a flamethrower!"

With the blank-faced zombie in front of me, I attempt to use my wrist device to order a flamethrower…

<Weapon Deployment Is Currently Restricted>

Gaaaaaah!

"Rose! Let's switch! I'm tagging out! I can't fight zombies! Switch out with me! Please!"

"B-B-Boss! Don't push me toward them! I-I'm actually not good with zombies, either…! My sense of smell is too strong! I think I'm gonna pass out…!"

Just then…

"Hold on. Leave this to me."

Wearing an unusually serious expression, Grimm gets up from her wheelchair.

"Hey, Grimm, what's going on? Acting cool won't make you stronger. There's no need to keep putting yourself on the line for the sake of a few laughs."

"Boss, don't spoil an opportunity for Grimm to shine. She's just excited because it's such a rare occasion."

"Shut up! Unless you two want to get cursed, just let me handle this." She begins walking barefoot on the soil, then turns toward us, her lips curled into a sad smile…

"I haven't told you yet, have I, Commander? …I…I, um…I'm not quite human anymore. I'm a bit like them, like the undead…"

"Ahhh, gotcha. So *that's* why you can regrow your head after it gets knocked off."

"I'm making a pretty big confession here! Can't you take this a little more seriously? Also, could you *not* treat my head like it's some lizard's tail? Anyway, let me handle them, okay?" Grimm huffs angrily as she approaches the zombies.

And then...

"Good evening... A lovely night, isn't it?" Grimm smiles gently at the rotting corpses, speaking to them as though greeting friends.

...Oh yeah, I guess Zenarith or whatever is in charge of the undead.

"Should be fine now, Boss. The undead actually like Grimm. She's probably got this."

"Are you sure? It's hard to imagine her being useful."

Leaving us to our conversation, Grimm walks up to the shambling horde with a serene smile on her face...

"Graaah!"

"Oof!"

...and ends up getting smacked across the face by a zombie.

"Huh?! G-Grimm, what just happened?! Oh! Boss, don't look at me like that. I wouldn't lie about that! She can usually talk them out of attacking! I swear! This is the first time I've seen this happen with her..."

Just seems like business as usual with Grimm to me.

"W-wait! I'm not your enemy! I'm Miss Grimm! Undead Idol! Ow! That hurt! H-how dare you do that to an Archbishop of Zenarith... C-Commander! Commander! Rose! Help!"

The self-professed Undead Idol is surrounded by zombies who begin beating the shit out of her.

"Why don't we start by burning them? Use your fire breath."

"Awww... But zombies smell *so* bad when you burn them..."

"A cute maiden's getting attacked by these abominations! Hurry up and help!"

I'd love to help her and all, but if I shoot the zombies surrounding her, I'll end up hitting Grimm as well.

Rose's flame isn't exactly precise, either. If she were to attack now, we'd end up with seven charred bodies.

"You know... I *really* don't want to hit those things with my bare hands. Can you get me a stick?"

"Understood. The smell makes it hard for me to get close. Can I leave them to you, Boss? ...Oh, hey, that's a weird-looking mushroom. I think I'll boil it as a snack when I get home."

"Forget it! I'll deal with them myself! Watch carefully. I'll show you the power of an archbishop! O Great Lord Zenarith! Remove your blessing of undeath from this place and return all things to how they should be!"

That is definitely the most magicy spell I've seen on this planet.

A blue-white magic circle appears on the ground, and light erupts toward the sky.

I briefly feel the presence of something otherworldly before it all scatters into the air, leaving silence in its wake.

Then the zombies who had been attacking Grimm freeze in place...

Like puppets suddenly cut free from their strings, the seven undead collapse to the ground.

"...Um, did our resident undead just kill herself?"

"...I hope the usual ritual can fix this..."

A few minutes outside the city, there's a cavern housing a shady-looking altar.

Rose and I have come to this cave to resurrect Grimm...again.

"I brought lots of offerings this time because of how she died. I hope it'll be enough..."

Rose looks uneasy despite the large number of sentimental objects before her.

"Considering the fact that she dispelled the blessing from her own god, yeah... If it were me, I'd just abandon her and forget the whole thing ever happened."

"Well, Grimm's been forgiven for dumb uses of her powers in the past. S-so I'm sure it'll be okay this time, too..."

I can tell she doesn't believe it, either.

The moonlight shines in from the hole in the center of the cavern, illuminating Grimm's body.

At the same time, the sacrificial offerings begin vanishing with flashes of light.

"Boss, looks like we're short on offerings, which is weird because I even threw in the love letter from her childhood friend that Grimm was so fond of showing off when she was drunk..."

"Ah, fine. I'll add a few, too..."

I take out my wallet and pull out some rare coins and a pachinko ball I kept as a good luck charm after a particularly large jackpot.

As the light consumes the items, Grimm's body twitches violently to life.

"Ah! Looks like that did it."

"...Uh, still seems like something's wrong."

Despite the movement, Grimm has yet to open her eyes.

"H-how dare you... Calling yourself Zenarith... Blasphemy... I'm a devout follower..." Grimm begins to mutter and moan, as if haunted by a nightmare.

"I bet you she's getting a lecture from her god."

"...This happens from time to time after Grimm dies in a stupid way..."

6

"Well, Boss, I'll take Grimm back to the barracks. She probably won't be up for a while, so I'll help you out tomorrow."

"Thanks. I'll leave you to it. She'll owe us big time when she wakes up."

Carrying the bundle of white flowers on her back, Rose disappears into the city, pushing the unconscious Grimm in her wheelchair.

After seeing Rose off, I head back to the hideout…

"…No one's home, I guess."

…or not.

I carefully glance around, then conceal myself among the shadows and head toward the castle…

"Looks like this year's Undead Festival's going to be bigger than usual."

"Makes sense. The battles against the Demon Lord's Army were pretty intense. But never mind that. Have you heard the rumors? About Her Highness? It seems she's been frowning in front of the rain artifact and…"

The night watch.

In front of the main gate, two soldiers trade gossip to pass the time as they stand guard.

I circle around the castle wall, moving to a spot the guards can't see. There's no need to go through the main gate to get inside, after all.

I place my compact pile driver against the wall and softly cover it with fabric.

It won't completely absorb the noise, but it's better than nothing.

I drive a stake into the wall, the muffled sound of impact echoing through the air.

The guards are too busy with their gossip to notice the noise.

I use the newly secured stake to climb over the outer wall and drop into the courtyard.

If memory serves, there are guard dogs being kept here, but I've come prepared with a secret weapon.

I acquired it after begging the mutant Tiger Man. "I knew you were weird, but I had no idea you were that much of a pervert," he told me. He even forgot to purr that time.

I take out the bottle and splash a few drops around...

"Arf, arf!"

"Whimper!"

I hear the frightened whining of dogs from a few feet away.

Yes, this is Tiger Man's pee. The dogs have caught the scent with their keen sense of smell and refuse to come closer out of fear.

Sneaking my way past the guard dogs, I reach my final obstacle. To get to the top of the castle, I'll have to climb this wall.

I whip out the pile driver again.

After a quick look around, I press it against the wall!

Careful to avoid making a sound, I remove the ceiling board and drop it quietly onto the carpeting below.

Lucky for me, the expensive-looking carpet does a good job of muffling any noise.

Arriving at my destination, I feel the thrill of excitement from pulling off a high-risk assignment.

<Large Sum of Evil Points Acquired>

Proof of my mission's success.

And there's the special announcement that I'll be getting a "large sum" of Evil Points.

I want to release some of this built-up tension, and fortunately, I have the perfect target in front of me.

*   *   *

"Mm…"

I hear a soft sigh in the dark room.

The sigh comes from the person in front of me: Tillis, this kingdom's princess.

Yes, I'm in Tillis's bedroom.

With Tillis fast asleep in front of me, I begin stripping off my power armor.

Careful not to wake her, I silently remove all my equipment.

I can feel my heart racing.

I worry for a moment that my rapidly beating heart will wake her, but judging by her peaceful breathing, it looks like I'm in the clear.

I can't hide a smirk at just how vulnerable she is.

After stripping off everything until I'm totally naked, I stare intently at the princess's sleeping face.

And begin doing squats right next to her.

7

I return to the hideout after completing my stealth mission with a nice workout in Tillis's room.

Despite the late hour, the light is still on in the workroom where Snow's been staying.

"Huh, she's still working? I figured she was just greedy, but I guess she's pretty dedicated when she wants to be," I murmur, and a familiar voice chimes in from behind me.

"Ah, Six, you're back. Snow's not the brightest, but she's also not that hard to understand. It makes her easy to manage. People motivated by money are pretty dependable when it comes down to it. Idealists who talk up stuff like sincerity and truth tend to lose sight of reality."

"You don't have to be so direct…"

She's got a thoroughly jaded view of human nature, but I suppose that's to be expected of an evil organization's android.

Alice is carrying a large bag, and I have no idea where she would have gotten it from at this hour.

"Tomorrow, we're going to start building a properly fortified fortress. Everything's going according to plan. Once the fortress is complete, we can start our conquest of the planet in earnest. Make sure you're ready, partner."

An unusually cheerful Alice throws encouragement my way as she watches the red shimmering outside the window.

If we succeed, I'll go from a permanent lackey to the proud owner of a fortress.

As a member of an evil organization, owning a lair to hunker down in and wait for the enemy is pretty high on the list of life goals.

Given that our competitors on this rock are holed up in a tower, I suppose it's one of those little universal chestnuts.

As the owner of a proper fortress, I'll become a mid-level villain, someone to be treated with respect and deference.

"Then it's almost time to say good-bye to this place, huh...? Given that this was our first hideout on this planet, I can't help but feel a little sentimental..."

"It's a bit of a pity, but the upkeep costs aren't trivial. I'm sure someone will grab it for a steal, but we're better off selling it. Then we will build an impregnable fortress."

As we sit contemplating the proper start of our conquest...

...our hideout explodes.

"How are you?"

Is everything going okay?

You've always been pretty reckless, so I can't help but worry.

I understand from Alice's reports that it's a very harsh world over there.

I would love nothing more than to send tons of weapons to support you, but unfortunately, the Heroes have staged a second counteroffensive on their home turf in America, and we can't spare the resources.

There might be things the locals eat that could be poisonous to humans.

Please make sure you check with Alice before eating anything.

Do take care of yourself.

I'm praying for your safe return.

Astaroth

PS: I saw from Alice's reports that you've added a maid-type Chimera to your ranks, but please be careful not to be fooled by some floozy.

Also, I've been meaning to bring this up, but it seems there are far too many women in your squa—

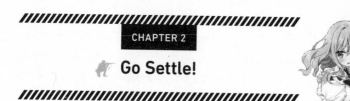

CHAPTER 2
Go Settle!

1

Having lost our hideout, we've set up tents in the Kisaragi territory we recently acquired from Toris as our temporary shelter.

I would have preferred an inn room or some place in the castle, but unfortunately, the recent drop in my reputation means all of them flat-out rejected me.

And now...

"Okay then, let's hear it."

Here in our temporary hideout, Alice begins interrogating Snow, who is sitting on the ground in a position of penitence.

"Yes, I did leave without putting the gunpowder away. And I apologize for bringing my newly acquired Flame Zapper the Second into the workplace. But please listen, Alice!"

"What did I tell you to call me while you owe me money?"

Snow bites her lower lip. "...Miss Alice."

"Good. Next time you forget, I'll start assuming you're as dumb as Six."

"P-please, anything but that!"

Hey!

"Well, *Miss* Snow, you don't seem all that sorry to me... Even *I'm* super careful when handling gunpowder. You've got a lot of nerve, making excuses after blowing all the blood, sweat, and tears we poured into our hideout sky-high."

"Says the man who didn't contribute a single thing when I funded that hideout," Alice quips, but I ignore her for now.

Unused to sitting on her knees, Snow's legs begin to tremble.

"Thanks to you, we're stuck camping out tonight. Me! The Grace branch manager of the Kisaragi Corporation! Reduced to living in a tent! You, my subordinate, are going to sleep under a roof while I'm stuck camping! Take responsibility, dammit! Specifically, let me stay in your house! And wait upon me hand and foot with your body!"

"Didn't you hate the words 'take responsibility'?" Alice is starting to get on my nerves with her constant quips.

With her numb muscles shaking, Snow raises her head. "They already evicted me from my house."

"...Huh?"

Snow's words catch me off guard.

"They evicted me because I couldn't pay my rent. There's no room in the castle barracks. That's why I've been sleeping on the sofa in your hideout. As such, I'm also camping out as of tonight."

"O-oh. Gotcha..."

I back up a little at Snow's serious expression.

"Heh-heh-heh... After steadily saving up for the down payment and taking out a long-term loan, I finally got Flame Zapper the Second... But she died in the blast...!" Snow mutters to herself, as though something inside of her has snapped, half sobbing, half laughing. "...You wanted me to serve you with my body, right? Fine! I don't care how much more I have to disgrace myself! Just let me stay in your tent! Please!"

Even I can't help but reel back as Snow pleads with a bow of her head.

Just how far does she plan to fall?

"There's no point in continuing to needle her. Besides, it's not that strange to lose a hideout or two to a freak explosion or whatever else. I'm also at fault for letting an amateur handle gunpowder. We're just lucky no one was hurt."

"Y-you're going to forgive me? After I blew up your home...?"

Alice smiles at Snow. "Of course. I won't abandon my employee. I'll provide you a place to stay and food as well. I also won't charge you interest on paying me back for the hideout. You mentioned your Flame Zapper the Second was destroyed in the explosion, right? I'll lend you the money if you're planning to buy a Third."

"L-Lady Alice...!"

Snow looks at Alice as one would a goddess.

Looks like this android plans to enslave this useless woman with debt.

Alice seems to be satisfied with pushing the cost of the old hideout on Snow instead of having to sell it after our fortress is complete.

"No use crying over spilled milk. Hey, Six, this is an emergency. We have to focus on building the new base. So forget about that stupid Undead Festival and focus on this instead," Alice says cheerfully, then claps me on the back.

"Sure, I've got this. I'm supercompetent, after all. I'll prove I'm not like that idiot over there."

"Y-you bastard! I'm going to be Lady Alice's right hand! I'll blow her away and get a raise!"

This bitch!

"If you want money that badly, go sell your body, you bum!"

"I'd have sold my body long ago if I could still ride a unicorn! My mount's been avoiding me ever since I kissed you! From now on, I'm going to charge you if you so much as look at my chest!"

Snow then puffs out her chest, making sure my eye is drawn in that direction.

"I'm Alice's partner, dammit! Don't try to usurp that position! I'll lose my allowance! Hrmph! Don't let the fact that you've got a huge rack go to your head! What—are you saying I can grope you if I pay up?"

"Hey, stop it! Don't try to grope me! It'll cost you! Touching will cost you! Stop! Stoppp—!"

Alice mutters as she watches Snow desperately fight off my grabbing hands.

"What's a droid gotta do to get some decent help around here...?"

2

Alice, Snow, and the two Chimeras are lined up in front of the massive pile of building materials sent from Earth.

Standing on a slightly elevated spot, I pick up the loudspeaker.

"Good morning, everyone! My name is Agent Six, manager for the Kisaragi Corporation's Grace Kingdom branch. Our mission will be to construct a fortress to serve as a base for our settlement of the Cursed Forest. Our land is plagued by environmental pollution and population growth, as well as food shortage. Humanity's future rests upon your shoulders..."

Today we begin construction on our fortress. Once we have a proper stronghold, I'll obtain the title of underboss, which is separate from positions like Supreme Leader.

Positions like Supreme Leader represent power, while titles like underboss represent accomplishments.

Of course, once I obtain the title, I'll be able to lord it over the other agents.

*   *   *

As I'm basking in the glow of this event and giving my speech, my heartless subordinates start complaining from the sidelines.

"What's the point of this? You're rambling and not making any sense! We're getting paid by results. Stop with the stupid speeches, and let's get started!"

"Boss! It's just weird when you start using big words out of the blue. Let's get this over with so we can go eat!"

These lackeys clearly need a lesson on the chain of command.

"Shut it! Once the fortress is complete, I'll be an underboss! That makes me important! I'll be much more important than you rank-and-file lackeys! You two better start treating me with respect!"

After I yell at them with the loudspeaker, Snow and Rose bristle.

"Who are you calling a lackey?! I'm still a knight of this realm! I'm here at Princess Tillis's orders, and I'm decidedly *not* a part of your shady organization!"

"That's right! Stop treating me like I'm part of your group!"

As I'm pondering how to quiet down the unruly pair, Russell sighs and pipes up. (I dragged him here due to a lack of personnel.)

"Hey, you know... I beat the crap out of you with my giant weapon. I'm only following you guys because Tiger Man is unreasonably strong. We Chimeras are closer to wild animals than humans, you know, so we'll follow someone stronger than us. I'm not going to take orders from a weakling like you."

...*Oh yeaaaah?*

"You've got some nerve, you brat, considering I took you down with a single shot! I'd be happy to come beat the shit out of you right now, you cross-dressing exhibitionist!"

"Th-that was a sneak attack from behind! And I'm not an exhibitionist! I'm not a pervert like you!"

At the word *exhibitionist*, Snow and Rose open a little distance between themselves and Russell.

"W-wait, Sis! He's lying..." Even Russell has a hard time being rejected by another Chimera, and he hurriedly begins making excuses.

"I'm sorry, Russell, but could you stop calling me Sis while you're dressed like that? It might not seem like it, but I'm still trying to take my life seriously."

"Rose, this cross-dressing brat is definitely on Six's end of the spectrum. You'll catch the stupidity if you spend too much time with him."

"Hold on! Just hold on a minute! I'm trying to live seriously, too! It's just that I got captured by a bunch of weirdos!"

As the three of them neglect me to yell among themselves, I let loose with the loudspeaker at close range.

"Bah! Why can't I get any good help? A cross-dressing Chimera, a gluttonous Chimera, and a cheap floozy. Try being in my shoes, attempting to build a fortress with help like you! Especially *you*, the one who blew up the hideout! You should be begging me for mercy each and every day!"

"You bastard, just who are you calling a 'floozy'?! I'll admit I'm cheap, but calling me a floozy is just your damned opinion! Also, there was a reason I was outside the hideout! Someone was looking in from the window..."

"Boss, calling a girl a 'gluttonous Chimera' is a little much, isn't it?! If you're going to call me a glutton, I'll go ahead and start gnawing on you, too!"

"Y-you lot are the ones making me cross-dress!"

With all three of them speaking up at once, I can't make out what they're saying.

However, it's easy enough to see they have no respect for their boss. I spit on the ground in front of them to let them know what I think of that.

"You idiots! You'll regret it when the fortress is done and I'm an underboss! Insubordinate lackeys like you will be on permanent shoulder-rubbing and toilet-cleaning duty. If you want to avoid that, get to work!"

"Rose! Russell of the Water! We'll surround this bastard and bury him in the forest! Underboss, shmunderboss! We'll get rid of this useless superior!"

"It hurts to have the boss—of all people—call me slow-witted."

"You *do* remember I'm a Chimera who used to be one of the Demon Lord's Elite Four, right? You really think a mere human can beat me in a fair fight?"

As the three of them start issuing threats, I smack my fist into my palm with a loud *thwack*.

"Yeah? Let's do this. You really think the three of you can take me in an actual fight? Come at me, you damned lackeys! I'll happily bring all of you to tears!"

"I'll go after his neck from the back," says Snow. "We'll form a triangle around him and attack him. Take your places!"

"I bet this battle was fated to happen before we were even born. I woke from my ancient slumber just for this day…," Rose murmurs.

"Ha-ha. I've needed a release after all the stress I've accumulated from being dressed up like this. I'll make you into my playthi— Ow, ow, ow, ow! Attacking me while I'm talking isn't fair… Wait! My arm doesn't bend that way!"

While Snow and Rose are rambling on about some nonsense, I take the opportunity to grab Russell's arm. The other two hurriedly try to help him, but I circle around behind Russell as he cradles his arm, putting him in a choke hold.

"Boss! Mr. Russell's foaming at the mouth! I think that's enough!"

"Stop! Let him go, Six! You're going to make your maid corps into a maid corpse!"

As I refuse to let go despite the blows to my head and back, Alice picks up the loudspeaker and, with a sigh, points it in my face.

"Listen up, Six! The longer it takes to build a fort, the longer we live in tents. Don't you want your own room? You can't enjoy porn without any privacy."

I freeze at Alice's words.

"Besides, Six wasn't exaggerating. If we successfully finish the fortress and settle the forest, it'll solve lots of problems. That'll make you lot heroes. You come to our world, you'll get a massive bonus and live a life of luxury… See? That's worth it, right? Good. Let's get to work!"

With a renewed sense of purpose, we steadily complete our tasks.

Using the heavy machinery acquired with Evil Points, we begin laying the foundation.

The forest stretches out near the planned fortress location. Everywhere else, there's nothing but wasteland.

Settling and developing the Cursed Forest: It's a grand project that'll solve the countless problems facing both this planet and Earth.

3

Both a scream and an explosion ring out in the wastelands near the Cursed Forest.

"Russell!"

Seems the cross-dressing Chimera just got caught in a blast.

One day after setting up the tents and beginning land development…

…we're currently being attacked by a herd of monsters.

"Lady Alice! Russell's hit! Save him, please! We can't afford to lose him yet!"

Evidently, Snow was the one who screamed earlier.

I didn't realize she and Russell were that close. I guess it pains her conscience because he looks like a child? Actually, the surprising thing has to be that the gold digger has a conscience to begin with.

"He's fine. I mean, wearing a maid outfit in a war zone isn't exactly normal, but Battle Chimeras won't die from a blast that weak. Give him a couple aspirin, and he'll heal eventually."

"O-oh, all right," she says. "Seeing how badly he gets treated, I'm relieved that someone has it worse than I do! I can't have him die here!"

Well, now I feel like an idiot for thinking positively of her.

Ignoring this worthless woman, I run toward the epicenter of the explosion.

"Targets are hostile mupyokopyokos. They appear to attack by self-destructing!" I yell out to Alice, then draw my gun, moving into effective range of the enemy.

Alice follows me with her shotgun in hand, also running. "Six, those are mipyokopyokos. Rookie mistake," she quips.

"That's right. Those are the ones that are too dangerous to eat. Please don't mix them up!"

"Who the hell cares?! Charge! Onward! Onward!"

At my order, we all rush in.

The targets are weird bipedal frog-faced creatures hopping around in front of us.

I fire off a shot at one of them, and it promptly explodes.

The others regard the creatures with caution as they tauntingly hop around.

"Hey, Alice, this is the seventh attack since we broke ground here! Do we *have* to build here? There's gotta be better spots than this!"

"This is the only land we acquired. Suck it up. If you don't like it, go invade the demon territory or Toris and get more land."

"What sadist came up with this game anyway?! Dammit!"

Just as I yell that out…

…Snow and Rose, who had been fighting the pyokopyokos, speak up with near panic in their voices.

"Six! There's supopocchis emerging from the forest! A herd of supopocchis!"

"There's a group of mokemokes coming, too! Boss, what do we do? I can't possibly eat this many!"

The constant reports of new hostile creatures are enough to tip me off that something's wrong here.

"Alice! Aliiiice! Is it normal for monsters to start attacking in droves because people try to settle in the forest?"

"Pay attention, Six, and look behind them. Bashin tribe members. They're clearly stirring up the monsters. That must be how they defend their territory. Fascinating!"

"Not fascinating! Frightening! We're getting out of here! Retreat!"

At my order, the others rapidly start pulling back.

Rose has already fetched Russell and carried him back without being told to do so. I can't quite decide if I should praise her initiative.

I've stayed behind to issue orders; during all this, a few of the supopocchis and mokemokes start heading toward me.

"Hey, where the hell is Tiger Man? This is the sort of thing we have mutants for, isn't it?"

"There's been border skirmishes with Toris. Tiger Man and the other agents are off dealing with them. They'll be back eventually."

Snow, who has been watching until this moment, draws her sword and steps in as though to cover Alice's back. "Ha-ha-ha-ha! Monster hunting is my specialty! Come at me, you walking bonus checks! Add to my income!"

At a glance, she looks like a knight defending the helpless, but the naked greed warping her smile ruins the image.

I fire off a shot at a nearby target, then land a front kick on a mipyokopyoko launching a jump kick at my flank.

"Even if we finish the base here, we'll just be dealing with constant monster attacks. Let's find another spot, Alice!"

"After all we went through to acquire this territory, we're not letting it go that easily. Never mind that, Six; cover your face. I'm going to blow up the mipyokopyoko you just kicked."

I throw my hands up to cover my face before Alice finishes speaking...

"Besides, if we're here, our research targets will be coming to us. I've managed to talk the leadership into giving us Evil Points if we send research samples to headquarters. So..."

Alice aims her shotgun.

"...this is your job from here on out. Wanna head back to Earth? Well, put your life on the line and earn us some points, partner!"

"Goddammit! Again?! I'm sick of busting my ass! Fine. I'll do it. I'll do it! I'll hunt! I'll misbehave! I'll save up my points and make those Supreme Leaders pay for it with their bodies!"

The mipyokopyokos' explosions echo through the wasteland.

4

Settling the frontier means a struggle against the natives.

Watching the forest from atop the construction site, I shout a warning.

"Alice! We've got more barbarians incoming!"

It's one day later.

Although we're eager to see an end to our camping-out status as quickly as possible and working on building an impenetrable fortress, we encounter a group of barbarians different from the Bashin tribe.

"Doesn't look like they're armed, and given their numbers, I'm sure Snow and Rose can handle them. Six, let's have you stay on watch duty. If we stop every time we're attacked, we're never going to finish this damn thing."

Alice says this from the operator chair of a crane, moving construction equipment into piles.

The group before us have tattoo-covered bodies, each member wearing only a wooden mask and a loin cloth.

Since our cross-dressing Chimera exploded the other day, we're down to four people at the construction site.

Still, this batch of barbarians doesn't appear to have any obvious weapons.

Like Alice said, Snow and Rose should be enough to chase them off.

As I'm pondering this, Snow, wearing a hard hat and wielding a pickax, looks up and comments, "Wait, that's the Hiiragi tribe! They value harmony and coexistence with nature! They use odd powers that are different from magic! They're not very dangerous to people, but they're extremely aggressive against invasive structures!"

"What do you mean 'odd powers'? Everyone on this planet is weird, if you ask me... Eh? What are they doing?"

It doesn't look like the tribesmen are going to attack the fortress I'm standing on. They're just observing us from a distance.

Retrieving drums and flutes, they then begin dancing to a mysterious tune.

"What should we do, Alice? They've started dancing. Should I go with the flow and join in?"

"What good would that do? Still, what *are* they doing? ...Wait, there's an excessive amount of sunlight shining in from above."

Light begins raining down upon the fortress from the sky.

Standing in the middle of that light, I feel like I'm being worshipped by the natives.

As soon as they see this, Snow and Rose toss aside their heavy pickaxes and start running for some reason.

"Wow, I'm totally shimmering. Hey, Alice, I feel like a god! Should I bestow some words of wisdom upon them?"

"Stop rambling like an idiot and get out of there. Everyone retreat!"

My legs begin moving before I have time to think.

Just as I frantically make my way out of the fortress—

—a shaft of light comes down from the sky, blowing off the top of the structure.

"Bwaaaaaaaaaaaaaah!"

Shielding my face from the debris, I see the Hiiragi tribesmen retreat toward the forest.

Alice stares up at the sky, head tilted.

"Was that a solar ray–style energy weapon? Odd, we didn't detect any satellites around this planet when we landed here."

"I bet that's just divine power of some sort! It's retribution for our blasphemy! Oh, gods, I'm so sorry! I'll stop robbing your collection boxes! I'll even reduce how often I harass your priestesses!"

As I pray, Alice begins sorting through the wreckage. "They usually use lightning for divine retribution. Look, some of the wreckage is melted. Safe to assume it's a heliostat of some sort. We can take precautions against that."

"C'mon, stop it! That's gotta be divine retribution! What do you plan to do if we keep blaspheming and get punished even worse?"

Just then...

"Oh! They're trying to run off with Mr. Russell!"

"W-wait, dammit! Despite his looks, he's a guy!"

I turn to see the Hiiragi tribesmen carrying off the unconscious Russell like he's the spoils of war.

Rose and Snow retrieve their pickaxes and give chase.

A few hours later.

I don't know exactly what happened in the forest, but Rose returns looking exhausted and carrying Russell and Snow, who are both out cold.

*   *   *

Settling the frontier is a struggle against nature.

In the middle of a giant sandstorm, Alice uses me as cover and yells, "Hey, Six! Pull harder! We'll lose the tent!"

In between repelling the attacks from the Bashin tribe, the Hiiragi tribe, monsters, and mokemokes, we've been steadily fortifying our base...

"What the hell is wrong with this planet's climate?! Not a cloud in the sky one moment and a giant sandstorm the next... Gah! Snow just got blown away!"

Snow, who had been barely weathering the intense gusts, is being carried off by the wind. She had initially taken off her heavy armor to make her construction work easier, but that apparently made her too light.

"Hey, Alice, I don't see the cross-dressing Chimera. Where'd he go?"

"Him? The first gust blasted him away, and now he's stuck in one of the trees. I've sent Rose to retrieve him. At any rate, forget about the tents, Six. We won't need them once the fortress is completed anyway. So long as you keep that stupidly heavy power armor on, you'll be fine. Let's get back to work," Alice remarks while operating heavy machinery.

"You sure we can keep working under these conditions? Whoa! Alice! The storm's blowing some dangerous stuff our way!"

Just as Alice jumps out of the cockpit, the partly constructed base and construction equipment explode.

The blast from the explosion and the sandstorm send an intense gale our way.

I look at the wreckage of the heavy machinery.

"Hey, Alice. If we keep spending Evil Points at this rate, I'm going to get arrested before we finish the hideout."

Currently, I'm only allowed to spend Evil Points for equipment and materials needed for the base.

Which means that I've been building up my Evil Points balance with steady effort every day after work, but...

"Just how are you earning all these points anyway? All this construction material and equipment. Did you end up committing some massive misdeed?" Alice asks the question as though it's been bothering her for a while.

"You worry too much. I'll tell you how I'm doing it once the hideout's complete. I can at least tell you I'm not doing anything dangerous."

"...Well, I already know you're not capable of anything too heinous, so I'm not worried about that..."

I've been pretty fond of infiltration missions lately, making use of the hard-won experiences from countless battles.

Basically, I've been sneaking into the castle every night to earn more Evil Points.

"It may not seem like it, but I'm pretty good at espionage..."

"Oh? Sounds like you're up to something a little more impressive than your usual misdeeds. I'm looking forward to learning more."

As Alice savors the thought, I give the order to retreat.

Really, at this pace, I have no idea how long it's going to take to finish this. I wanted to keep all the credit for my unit, but that's no longer a luxury I can afford. "Guess we may as well put all our effort into this. Let's recall some of the agents deployed to the front and focus on getting this base done first. Should be easy once we properly commit Kisaragi's efforts to it."

"You really do love tempting fate, don't you...?" Alice mutters with an exasperated expression as I gain confidence in our chances of victory.

5

Settling the frontier is…

"Screw this place! I'm going back to Earth!"

"I understand how you feel, Six, but calm down. If you return to Earth with a negative point total, you'll get punished. More importantly…"

Alice looks at the things surrounding us.

"So these are the zombies you mentioned. Wonder how they're moving? Are they animated by some sort of parasites? Or maybe they're robots on the inside…?"

"Forget about the analysis and do something about them!"

As our fortress approaches completion, a horde of zombies has emerged from the forest to surround it.

The other agents are here today, but these odds aren't good.

Upon closer inspection, it's clear I'm not the only one afraid of zombies.

Rose and Russell, the Chimera pair with a keen sense of smell, are frozen by the awful stench. And all the other agents have no motivation to fight.

"Fighting's the whole point of being an agent, isn't it? Why are you all cowering back here anyway?"

"Zombies are our natural predators. You've seen zombie movies, right? Guys like us are the first to die. The more zombies you kill, the more gruesome your fate. Then there's the fact that they splatter when you shoot them. That's pieces of rotting human. Pretty sure my appetite's gone for the night if I see that."

As we're caught up in debate, the horde of zombies begins climbing over the fence.

Just then, Snow inserts herself between the zombies and the rest of us, staring them down.

"Hrmph! How pathetic. Shambling zombies are no match for my blade."

Despite her usual uselessness, Snow makes her declaration with an inspiring bit of confidence. But she keeps casting small glances toward Alice...

"Fine, fine. If you beat them, you can have a bonus. Our Combat Agents are apparently afraid of dumb superstitions. And they're supposed to be evil henchmen? Pathetic. You damn chickens!"

Snow rushes in, letting out an odd cry of happiness at those words.

"Don't call us chickens!" I snap at Alice. "Our evil nature is what makes us afraid. If there's zombies and ghosts, that means there's an afterlife. Given how much evil we've done, that means we're all headed straight to hell. That's why we Combat Agents are so hard to kill and cling so hard to life."

"If you're a Kisaragi Combat Agent, you should be treating hell like another place to conquer. But at this rate, we're never going to finish our construction," Alice says, looking over to Snow.

Motivated by the prospect of a bonus, Snow is wreaking havoc among the rotting zombies, ignoring the spray of rotting blood and flesh.

"Looks like she's completely given up on being a woman..."

"Combat Agents should be like that. You're less useful than the natives."

Snow's returning the zombies to their maker using a flaming magic blade; that must mean she's bought her Flame Whatever III.

Although she's rarely much use against powerful enemies, I guess she wasn't a knight captain for nothing. She's making quick work of the zombies.

A truly momentous occasion. We should give her a little encouragement.

"Good work, Snow! Just what we'd expect from Grace's greatest swordswoman! We can't handle zombies! I'll let Tillis know you are worth your weight in gold!"

"...?! T-truly?! You better be serious! Feel free to exaggerate the number of zombies in your report, too!" Encouraged by my words, Snow continues her rampage, eyes glittering happily.

And it seems she's come to the conclusion that her armor is just weighing her down against the slow zombies, unfastening her equipment to lighten her load.

With each swing of her sword, the boob knight places more and more emphasis on showing off her assets, leading my coworkers to enthusiastically cheer her on.

"Good work, otherworlder! You're awesome!"

"I'm impressed! I owe you a drink later!"

"Keep the show going!"

Snow, aware of the skills of the average Kisaragi Combat Agent through regularly interacting with us, looks surprised at the praise they're giving her.

Eventually, she begins to smirk...

"Tsk, it's just zombies, boys! Leave them to me! You can just watch from over there!"

"Whoa! Look at that!"

"What a sight! She's at least Lady Astaroth...no, Lady Belial class!"

Thoroughly egged on by the cheering, Snow eliminates the zombies, returning with a satisfied expression on her face.

"To cower in front of mere zombies in spite of your usual strength, sheesh! All right! If you ever run into zombies, leave them to me! I'll wipe them out for you!"

Alice and I head over to welcome the giddy Snow back.

"Good work, Tittania."

"I'm impressed, Tittania. I'll make sure you get an extra bonus."

"Stop calling me that! …Say, Six, I wanted to ask you. What did my admirers mean when they said I was Lady Belial class…?"

"Lady Belial is one of my superiors and one of our Supreme Leaders. She's the head of Kisaragi's combat division and possesses the highest power level in our organization."

She's also got the biggest cup size in Kisaragi.

"Th-they think I'm equal to such a person? I feel like that's a bit of an exaggeration… B-but it's not a bad feeling."

Tittania smirks, evidently quite pleased at being compared to someone like that.

"I feel it's a fair comparison. Given your age and growth potential, you're perfectly in Lady Belial's class."

"Y-you think so? Well, if you're willing to go that far. I—I mean, I did climb to knight captain. I'm pretty confident in my blade skills."

Tittania, who is actually pretty easy to manipulate, happily swings her sword around.

Just then…

"We've got a fresh batch! Hey! We've got another load of zombies coming out of the forest!" shouts the Combat Agent keeping watch on the forest.

Looking over in that direction, I catch sight of a few hundred zombies emerging from the forest heading straight to the hideout…!

"All right, it's time for you to shine. Go show us what you're made of!"

"Don't be ridiculous! I can't handle *that* many. Let me in!"

Quickly giving up on stopping the zombies, Snow starts yelling and rattling the fence surrounding the hideout.

"Of course you disappoint the moment I have a little faith in you. You're as useless as ever, Tittania!"

"That's fine! I'll be Tittania! Just let me in! Please! There's way too many of them!" Tittania pleads tearfully.

"Ohhh? Seems you've finally come to terms with your worth, eh?

Well, in that case, I suppose I can help you. But listen. You better treat me with the respect due to a superior. Second, you better obey my orders! When I say show off your boobs, you bend forward, got it? Next..."

...?

I swear there's an animal suit out there in the forest.

No, wait, that's a giant cat plushie...

Just as I narrow my eyes and focus my gaze to get a better look in that direction...

"Hey, Six! You staying behind? We're ditching this place for now! Get a move on!"

...Alice calls out to me from a distance, as I'd stayed at the hideout to taunt Snow.

...A distance?

"Wait, you're all out already?! Snow, you're supposed to be a knight, right? Hold them off for us!"

"I'm a woman before I'm a knight! I totally wouldn't mind if you let me leave first! You should hold them off!"

"Don't try to play the woman card at times like this! Alice, help!"

6

It's the day after we abandoned fortress construction and returned to town.

Alice is pissed off because of all the delays.

We're currently occupying the city's park and have turned it into a temporary base.

Obviously, they'd yell at us if we built an actual base there, so we just set up a bunch of tents.

"Okay, time to rethink our plan. Sorry, Six, I haven't been taking this planet seriously enough. I didn't expect to fail with this many Combat Agents involved. This is on me," Alice says as I finish putting up my tent.

Given her usual confidence, it's weird for her to be so contrite.

Alice spreads out a map of the surrounding area, kneeling down in front of it. "I chose that land for our base because I thought it would let us watch over Toris and our competition while gathering samples from the forest. But it's time to stop being so greedy. We'll wait till things calm down a bit before sending a unit to collect samples."

"I was hoping that having the forest nearby would let us eat mokemokes whenever we wanted. So if we're giving up on the forest, are we moving our base location?"

Alice shakes her head in response. "Let's burn down the forest. That'll throw the natives and fauna into a panic. We can use that time to finish construction."

I can't shake the feeling that this new approach seems a little extreme. If this planet had any environmental groups, they'd be coming after us with torches and pitchforks. I mean, arson *is* every villain's dream, but...

"The Cursed Forest spans most of the continent. Reducing a woodland that size to ash would take a long, long time. After a large-scale bombing or fire, the air gets filled with soot and ash, which leads to cloud formation and rain. Keep that in mind. A forest that big won't be reduced to wasteland just from a little fire—go burn to your heart's content."

"I suppose flamethrowers would make it easier to deal with the zombies, too... And so long as it's a forest fire..." I look to my side. "...We can have him handle fire suppression."

"...I mean, sure, I'm good with water magic, so firefighting would be something I could handle, but...listening to your conversation makes me think you guys are a lot more of a threat to humanity than us demons could ever hope to be."

There's a hint of exasperation in Russell's tone as he busily prepares everyone's meals over the stove he built next to the tents.

With the Cursed Forest before us, Alice calls out to the group.

"Are you ready, you bastards? We're an evil organization! Leave your morals at the door! Raze that forest to the ground—zombies, mokemokes, mipyokopyokos, and all!"

"""""WHOO-HOO!"""""

The Combat Agents let out a cheerful whoop.

You shouldn't join an evil organization if you're afraid of a little environmental destruction.

With each of them equipped with a flamethrower, all Combat Agents other than me let loose a stream of fire toward the forest. Even Rose gets swept up in the moment and joins in the festivities, adding her flame breath to the mix.

As the wet trees start bursting into flame, the forest—ever the perpetual thorn in our side—begins to go up in smoke.

I bet my coworkers are going to earn a lot of Evil Points for this assignment.

Flamethrowers are an evildoer's dream weapon.

I watch my coworkers happily engaging in arson and mumble...

"*Sigh*, if only I was allowed to order weapons, too..."

"You Combat Agents have a weird attachment to flamethrowers."

Just as I'm enviously watching my coworkers commit a grand act of arson...

"Hey! What are you doing to the forest?"

...a voice calls to us from behind, interrupting my and Alice's observations.

It's Snow, galloping toward us on a unicorn after seeing the black smoke rising from the forest.

I turn to Snow with my best evil grin. "What does it look like? We're burning down the forest. We're an evil organization. The ends always justify the means! If it's gonna mess with our base construction, we'll reduce the whole thing to ash!"

"You're showing off now," Alice retorts, "but you were the one who was worried about taking things too far."

"There's no time for your petty banter! Hurry and retreat. The forest is about to retaliate."

...The forest can retaliate?

"Gaaaahhhh?! B-Boss! BOSS!!"

I turn toward the sudden scream and see Rose hanging upside down in the air, a root holding her up by her ankle.

Meanwhile, the Combat Agents, myself included, gather around her.

"H-hey?! Wh-why are you just watching instead of helping?"

We settle down in a spot under Rose, sitting on the ground and gazing up serenely.

As the announcements of Evil Point acquisition chime in our heads, Rose takes in a deep breath, holding up her skirt as gravity tries to peel it away—

"W-wait, hold on! We'll get you down, so don't use your breath!"

The other Combat Agents scatter as Rose prepares to strike.

Using my R-Buzzsaw, I prepare to hack away at the roots grabbing Rose...

"B-Boss! Behind you! Look behind you!"

"Hmm? Whoa! The hell is this?!"

Turning around, I see the ground shift and wriggle around me. Roots are starting to pop out here and there; this must be what Snow meant by the forest retaliating.

"Keep burning, boys! Use your flamethrowers from a distance and burn the damned things away!"

I give the orders as I jump to safety, but the ground beneath the Combat Agents swells as though it's about to explode…!

"Ahhhhhhhhhhhhhhh!"

"Wh-whoa! Th-this thing's trying to strip away my power armor! Stop! I'm not an exhibitionist like Six!"

"There are tons of pretty girls around here! Why are you attacking me?! Pay attention, dammit!"

Reduced to a struggling mass, the Combat Agents fight against the roots tangling around them.

Although the strength boosts from the power armor are letting them resist the roots, the flamethrowers aren't much use against the ones that approach from underground.

As if mocking our confusion, the trees begin spraying a mist from their leaves.

"…This planet's flora comes with its own fire-suppression abilities?" observes Alice from a distance. "That's incredibly fascinating."

"This is hardly the time for observations! We're outmatched! Let's get outta here!" I yell as I chop up the roots holding Rose with my R-Buzzsaw.

Just then, we hear a high-pitched scream.

"Gyaaaaaaaaaah!"

I look over and see our resident firefighter, Russell, getting snatched up by a bunch of roots.

"You know… He kinda looks like a pretty maid getting groped by tentacles, but he's still got a dick…"

"Would you stop with the weird comments? The forest is only getting started! We should get out of here while it's occupied with Russell!"

Snow offers a harsh proposal, but Alice holds up her hand to shoot it down.

"I'm all for running, but go cut down one of the trees. There's something I want to try."

7

A good distance away from the forest, we slump onto the ground, exhausted. Alice uses points from the other Combat Agents to order a variety of chemicals from Earth. She appears to be experimenting with the tree we'd grabbed on the way out.

I settle next to Alice and watch her work. "What are you up to this time?"

"Trying out various defoliants. Looks like they work on this planet's plants, too. If these didn't work, I was going to have them send me viruses tailored for plant use."

No biological weapons. Ever.

"Hey, Alice, are you sure these defoliants are safe? They're not poisonous to humans, are they?"

"We've come a long way since Vietnam. Kisaragi Corporation defoliants break down and become harmless after a month. They only use natural ingredients, so they're even safe to drink."

That actually sounds pretty shady.

"All right, we'll dispense it using drones. Make sure you're somewhere safe, just in case."

"Hey, you're sure this stuff *is* safe, right? What do you mean 'just in case'? Didn't you say it was okay to drink?"

Alice ignores my concerns, quickly loading the defoliant onto a drone.

And then—

"Hey! That weird thing just started flying! Boss, what is that?!"

"Wow! It's flying! Flying!"

Excited by the foreign tech, the two Chimeras watch the drone with rapt attention.

"That's a drone. It's an unmanned plane that Alice controls with her remote... Hey! What are you doing?! Don't try to shoot it down!"

The drone seems to trigger the Chimeras' predator instincts.

I manage to stop them just as they start grabbing rocks and throwing them at the drone.

"Six, keep those two on a leash, will you? We'll try dispersing the defoliant with a single drone. If it works, we'll use a fleet of them and get this taken care of," Alice says as she sends the drone to hover over the forest.

The drone begins dispersing defoliant…

With a *bang*, the drone disappears.

"The weird thing's gone."

"Whoa! It vanished in a blink of an eye! Drones are awesome!"

It really seems to have stirred up something inside the two as they keep chattering excitedly.

"Drones don't just vanish! Hey, Alice, something just sniped the drone!"

"Wait, that's…"

Before Alice can finish speaking, the forest suddenly splits open.

The rock-hard trees give way…

I let out a loud cry.

"It's a beautiful girl! A beautiful, naked girl just popped out of the ground! This planet's got trees that grow beautiful girls! Hooray!"

"Hooray for new worlds!"

"Hooray for beautiful girls!"

A beautiful girl, growing out of the bushes, smiles over at us. Her body is wrapped in budding vines.

The vines are covering her most sensitive spots, but the look is actually more erotic than if she were just plain naked.

The green-haired girl points a finger at us as we stand there cheering.

"Get it together, you meatheads; that's a hostile life-form! It probably has some sort of projectile weapon." Alice ducks behind me and issues a warning to the Combat Agents.

The green-haired girl pointing her finger toward us lets out a soft chuckle and the tips of the buds suddenly face us—

"Ow, ow, ow, ow, ow! Wait, this stuff hurts even through the power armor! It'll split your head open like a pomegranate if you're not careful!"

I throw my hands up to guard my face as a bunch of hard objects are thrown in my direction.

Alice yells out again from behind me. "Retreat! Deploy riot shields and retreat!"

"Wait! I can't order a riot shield with my equipment restrictions! Someone shield me, please!"

I glance around with my arms still guarding my face and only see my coworkers backing away under the cover of their shields.

Snow and Rose were standing near me just a moment ago, but they appear to have made a run for it the moment the forest split open.

"The equipment! Use the equipment for cover! Even that won't damage a power shovel…"

As I retreat toward the construction equipment, the green-haired girl smiles again.

"Aahhhh! Alice! Aliiiice!"

"Calm down, Six. She's no different from the mutant Two-Mouthed Woman."

The top of the girl's head pops open like a blossom, and then she turns to the equipment.

It looks like she's preparing to launch another attack like the flower buds from earlier.

The construction equipment rings as though hit by a bullet, then tips over onto its side. There is a huge dent in its frame.

Then the equipment's gas catches fire, and black smoke begins rising from it.

Staring at it, Alice and I mutter:

""Let's go home.""

8

Reoccupying the park and setting up our tents and fire pits as our hideout (temporarily), we settle down to rest our tired bodies.

It's the middle of the night, and everyone is fast asleep by the time I'm able to crawl out of my tent.

It all just started on a whim. Something I came up with by chance.

I just wanted to surprise her while she slept. But now it's escalated, and I can't figure out how to stop. I'm well aware of the consequences if I get caught. Everything I've worked to establish will come crumbling down overnight.

But I can't afford to stop now.

Looking over at the tents where everyone is sleeping, I nod.

Off I go...

With the moon out tonight, the spot where I drove my stakes in last time is brightly lit.

I can't use the same route this time.

But that's where the Kisaragi power armor comes in.

Careful to avoid the guards, I get a running start and jump.

Thanks to the power armor's assistance, I manage to grab hold of the top of the outer wall.

Ordinarily, I'd use my stake gun to climb the rest of the way, but adaptability is the name of the game for infiltration missions.

Dropping into the courtyard, I spray Tiger Man's scent like last time...

"Have you heard the rumors? Evidently, someone in an animal suit is causing trouble in the city. There hasn't been much damage yet, but I hear it's a little different from the usual stuff."

"Those scary stories are pretty common this time of year, though. Nothing particularly weird about a doll going on a rampage. But never mind that; did you hear? One of the cleaning girls mentioned it, but evidently they've noticed a man's scent in the princess's bedroom. Could it be that the princess is sneaking someone into her room...?"

Maids on the night shift exchange gossip as they make their way down the hall, while I duck under some bushes.

I'm tempted to follow the maids, but that's not why I'm here tonight.

Of course, my destination is—

<Large Sum of Evil Points Acquired>

At the announcement of a massive point gain, I'm overcome with emotion.

She looks so innocent...

Her typically grown-up expression and smile have melted away, and the Tillis in front of me wears a youthful expression as she sleeps.

She is a young woman who bears the weight of this country on her shoulders with her political skill, a figure admired for taking on the burdens of running the country in her unreliable father's stead.

Next to a national treasure, I strip my power armor off, and—

Careful not to make any noise, I begin assembling my Jenga set near the sleeping Tillis.

"I Have New Underlings!"

Hi Agent Six,

How are you?

I am doing well.

The daily battle against the Heroes rages on. Each day is a new struggle.

Astaroth has been reading your reports, getting more frustrated and worried each time.

The Heroes know that I can't attack animals, so they've brought in a strong panda-shaped hero from China. It is really unfair.

Some new underlings showed up at my house.

They keep saying odd things just like you.

I bet you would like them.

I will introduce you to them when you get back to Earth.

I hope you come home soon.

Belial

1

"What's a sexy thing like you doing drinking all by yourself? Come over here and pour me a glass, would ya?"

"Wh-who are you? P-please leave me alone!"

With our fortress construction at a standstill, we've been reduced to spending our days drinking at dive bars around town.

"Never mind that—just come on over! I promise I won't try anything funny. I'm just offering to buy you dinner!"

"N-no way! You can't fool me! You have no intention of stopping with just dinner!"

It's not like I'm actually trying to pick her up. I'm just trying to let off some steam and earn some Evil Points in the process.

Which is why I'm drinking by myself and chatting up a random stranger...

"Relax, lady. I just want you to eat a little bit of this thing here. Mokemoke with a special thick milk sauce! Heh-heh, I'll treat you to it if you'll come over and pour my drinks for me! There's more, if you want it!"

"Lies! I bet when I finish eating, you'll next go, *Now you can have my special thick milk for dessert*, and do terrible things to me! You can't fool me!"

Holy shit, what a thing to say in public!

"N-no, that's something a dirty old man would say… I just need you to resist a little while eating some mokemoke. Go on; open your mouth."

"No way! I don't believe you! You'll say that as you force-feed me that sticky white stuff, and when my face is all messy, you'll start getting horny and say, *Next let's have your other mouth* eat *this*…"

"What the hell are you talking about? W-wait a minute. I haven't been getting any Evil Points this whole time! Now that I think about it, I recognize you!"

I can't remember where, but I can swear I've seen this woman before.

"Woe is me! After having his way with me, this man, becoming addicted to my body, is going to lock me up in a gorgeous lake house… And then he'll force me to have babies one after another, and after several decades, I'll happily draw my last breath, watched over by all my grandchildren…"

"Whoa, I'm not gonna do any of that! Are you even listening to me?! Forget it! I'm letting you go! Get outta here!"

"Noooooooooooo! After all this anticipation, you're just going to let me go? Noooooo! You're going to abandon me again after threatening to show me something in a dark alley?!"

"H-hey now, you're giving people the wrong idea! I'll pay your tab, so just leave me alone, please!"

Oh crap, I really stepped in it this time.

Just then…

…as I'm busy trying to pay off the weird woman's tab, a voice calls out to me.

"There you are. You're a hard man to find, Commander… Look, he's with me. Shoo!"

Shooing away the weirdo with a glare is an obnoxious woman driving her wheelchair into a crowded bar.

After watching the weirdo click her tongue in disappointment and head out the door, Grimm turns to face me.

"Tch, I can't leave you alone for a minute without you chatting up other women. Commander, are you a womanizer?"

"I won't deny that I'm surrounded by women, but they all come loaded with baggage."

"I guess you have problems of your own, Commander. But if you'll pick up the tab, I'm happy to go on a date with you whenever you want."

You've got the most baggage of any of 'em.

"Anyway, this most recent resurrection sure took a while, huh?"

"That's right. I remember purging the gift of undeath from the zombies, but I can't remember how I died. Then, while dead, I dreamed of a strange woman calling herself Lord Zenarith and yelling at me."

Was that really a dream? Maybe she was getting lectured in the afterlife?

Is she actually an archbishop?

"What is it? You look like you have something you want to say... Anyway, Commander, is it true? That you couldn't finish your base? And that you've got nothing to do?" Grimm chirps, gazing expectantly at me.

"Actually, I'm planning to gather scrap materials with some homeless guys tomorrow. It's pretty profitable. I'm broke after using up the allowance Alice gave me."

"Please don't resort to something so embarrassing! Wait. If you're broke, how were you planning to pay for the tab here?"

"I'm pretty quick on my feet, you know. I can outrun a bartender easily enough."

"You know, I'm still technically part of the army. I can't let you dine and dash in front of me! Tch, fine..."

As Grimm takes out her wallet and pays the tab, I head out of the bar.

Picking that joint was a mistake. Seems it's that weird woman's haunt. Guess I'll go elsewhere next time.

As I wander aimlessly, looking for the next bar, something bumps into me from behind.

"Why did you leave without me?! Hmph, to disappear without so much as a word of thanks after making a woman pay!"

The bump came from Grimm.

"Thanks for picking up the tab."

"You're welcome! Anyway, Commander, do you have a minute? I've got something pretty important to ask you."

Grimm wheels herself along next to me with an unusually serious expression on her face.

"I'm about to head to a second bar. If you're okay with that, we can chat."

"Why are you going if you're broke?! ...*Sigh*, this last resurrection was pretty pricey, too..." Grimm sighs as she looks sadly at the contents of her wallet.

"Considering you spend your free time harassing couples, I wouldn't expect you to be so serious."

"Harassing couples is the responsibility of every Zenarith follower. Say, Commander, I'll pick up your tab if you'll listen to me. There's something odd in the air lately."

Well, yeah...

"It's spring on this planet, right? Love is in the air, and couples are all getting it in while the getting's good. Like those two over there." I point to a couple.

"No, that's not what I meant! ...You two! Stop with the public displays of affection! I'll curse you!" Grimm threatens them. "The zombies we ran into... There was something odd about them."

With that, Grimm furrows her brow in as serious an expression as I've ever seen from her.

2

Grimm leads us to a fancy little spot that I'd never go into by myself.

In a space lit with gentle blue-white lighting, the patrons sip from colorful cocktails.

"As I was saying, Commander. I'm a friend and ally to the undead. But they refused to listen to me. As though someone else was controlling them…"

"Bartender, can I get another one of those pink drinks? Also, could I get something substantial to snack on?"

I put in some additional orders as Grimm swirls her cocktail glass with an expression of concern.

There's a high percentage of women among the patrons, and I can't resist glancing this way and that.

I gulp down the pink cocktail that's set down in front of me, then stuff something resembling a scone into my mouth.

I wonder how many Evil Points I'd earn if I got drunk enough to strip naked in the middle of the room.

"…This is a pretty serious problem with the Undead Festival right around the corner. Call it an archbishop's intuition, but I think something bad is going to happen at the festival."

"Bartender, another one of the pink ones. Also, something a little stronger. One of those brown drinks suited for an interesting man like myself."

It's not like I can drink a whole lot, but the enhancement to my ability to process poisons means I sober up quickly. Given that Grimm's paying, I decide to give that brown stuff a try.

"…C-Commander? Don't order too much, okay? My wallet's a little thin this time of the month and… Are you listening to a word I'm saying?"

"I'm listening, I'm listening. Snow got so desperate for cash that she made a mold of her breasts, and now she's selling the pudding she made with it, right?"

"Where did *that* come from? Also, make sure you don't mention that to Snow. She might be desperate enough to try it!"

It isn't my best moneymaking scheme, but I bet it'd sell well with morons.

Maybe I *will* propose it to Snow next time I see her.

"Bartender, can you send that really pretty lady a cocktail? Tell her it's from this customer here."

"Do you mind doing that with your own money instead of mine? Also, don't hit on someone when you've got a good woman like me sitting right next to you!"

The brown stuff smells really strong, enough to give me pause. While I hesitate, Grimm grabs me by the shoulders and shakes me.

"All right, fine. Grimm, this one's on me. Give it a try."

"Don't order it if you can't drink it! Commander, listen seriously, will you? The reason they keep me employed in this kingdom is to run the Undead Festival. That's what's paying for these drinks!" Grimm pleads desperately.

"Calm down a little. We're an evil organization. Trouble is our business. Our standard MO is to get involved with a problem, claim damages, and make money out of it. Also, leave the festival to us. Festivals mean stalls. Stalls means Kisaragi. From administration to protection money, we've got a perfect manual for this sort of thing."

"Wait, I don't remember joining any evil organization... Also, the Undead Festival—it's a holy event. It's not a moneymaking scheme," Grimm says with a look of concern.

Meanwhile, the woman at the end of the bar who got my cocktail from the bartender starts glancing in my direction.

It looks like he did the whole *It's from the customer over there* thing, as requested.

The bartender whispers something to the lady...

…who then stares intently at Grimm, her cheeks flushing red.

"…Commander, that woman's looking at me for some reason…"

I ask the returning bartender what exactly he said.

"As it appears your companion is paying, I handed her the cocktail and said, 'It's from the young woman over there'…," he replies.

"What?! It feels like she's staring at me rather intently. I hope she's joking… Wait, she's coming this way!"

Draining my cocktail, I turn to Grimm, who's starting to panic.

"Thanks for an interesting evening, in more ways than one."

"Why are you trying to leave on your own?! Commander, wait! Don't leave me here!"

Leaving Grimm behind and making my way back to the hideout, I run into a coworker preparing to head out despite the late hour.

The coworker in question is Agent Ten.

He's the second-longest-serving Combat Agent on this planet after me, and the others hold him in high regard for a variety of reasons.

Agent Ten double-checks his equipment with a serious expression on his face, and a single glance confirms to me he's on the same quest as I am.

Careful not to wake the others, Ten and I nod to each other in silence.

Tonight's a rare overcast evening on this planet.

Perfect weather for getting work done—

"Six to Ten. Two guards up ahead—caution recommended. Stakes are positioned on the outer castle wall. They're tricky to use on a clear night but should be an ideal route given the cloud cover tonight. Over."

"Ten to Six. I've dug an infiltration tunnel beneath the outer wall. Will use stake route tonight, but feel free to use the tunnel on a clear night. Over."

Ten and I exchange useful information over our infiltration headsets—a must-have item for mass stealth missions.

Given we're within three feet of each other, we don't really need to use them, but it helps set the mood for the mission.

Approaching my usual stakes at a crawl, I glance around and signal the all clear.

Placing my hands on the stakes in the wall, I feel a push at my feet and a sudden reduction in my weight. I don't need to look to know there's someone behind me.

Ten has wordlessly approached and lifted me to make it easier to climb the wall.

I feel reassured just by having the presence of a skilled comrade who works well with me on a mission like this.

I grasp the top stake with my right hand, lift my body, and hold out my left hand.

Ten grabs my hand, and together we clamber the rest of the way over the wall.

As Ten and I enter the courtyard, I reach into my jacket and retrieve the bottle as usual.

The contents are running a little low, so I need to ask Tiger Man for a refill. Honestly, I'd prefer not to since he gives me odd looks when I ask, but...

Ten wags his finger at me, as though to tell me to hold off on using the bottle, and instead shows off a wrapped paper package with a triumphant look.

Along with the package, he takes out some sort of meat, and based on its coloration, I can tell it's one of my favorites: mokemoke meat.

As he rubs the contents of the paper package on the meat, I realize he plans to use a sedative.

He's planning to combine a luxury food item like mokemoke meat with fast-acting sedatives that cost a ton of Evil Points.

"Whooo."

"Heh, oh stop..."

I tease Ten and his high-rolling tactics with a low whistle, and he responds with a faint smirk.

After a moment, Ten hurls the mokemoke meat in the direction from which the dogs have been released, holding his breath and ducking behind cover—

"Bark, bark, bark!"

"Awooo! Awooo!"

"What the hell?! What is it?"

"It's the hounds. Is there an intruder?"

Seems the dogs didn't like the mokemoke meat and are making a fuss.

"What the—?! Ten, you moron! Why were you acting so cocky earlier?"

"It worked last time. I guess those dogs are in the mood for supopocchi meat tonight. Anyway, let's get out of here. Come with me, Six."

Should I really be following him?

Despite the circumstances, Ten remains oddly cocky, leaving me wary even as I follow him.

"What the hell is up with your pack anyway? Couldn't you have packed a bit lighter?"

"This is all necessary equipment. You'll see when we get there. Worry about that later. Just use this for now."

Ten activates his optical camo device, then tosses one to me. This little gizmo uses an electromagnetic field to bend light, making you invisible to the naked eye at anything other than close range.

Ten uses this sort of expensive equipment with abandon, which makes me wonder how exactly he's earning the requisite Evil Points.

"I've always wanted to ask, how the heck do you get so many Evil Points? You're one hell of a high roller."

"I've got a younger sister going through her rebellious phase. So I get points just by hiding in her closet, eating her underwear as tempura, or pooping in her room."

"Ah, gotcha. Not something I can copy, then..."

I activate the camo device, then start spritzing around Tiger Man's pee to keep the dogs away.

Another night, another safe entry.

<Large Sum of Evil Points Acquired>

Once again, I hear the announcement of massive point gains as Tillis sleeps peacefully in front of us.

I've always wondered just how the Evil Point system works. Not earning points if the target consents and the point gain going down if you repeat the same action—the standards all seem a bit murky.

Ten and I nod to each other, then begin stripping off our power armor.

"Six, put this over there, will ya?"

As I relax in my T-shirt and shorts, Ten strips completely naked, then takes something out of the pack he's been carrying.

It's a portable air filter that removes odors from the air. Typically, it's used along with a portable ashtray when smoking.

I figure Ten is going to light up while watching Tillis sleep, but instead he produces a portable grill.

At this point, even I can figure out what the plan is for tonight.

We're going to have a barbecue here.

"Ten, you're insane. Grilling meat in front of a sleeping girl? What sort of brain comes up with this sort of thing?"

"I'll take that as a compliment. Check this out; it's a lightless heating coil—it doesn't glow. I brought a bunch of mokemoke meat, too. This meat's priceless in situations like this because it doesn't make any noise when cooking."

I somehow doubt this is a situation we'll find ourselves in again, but it's pretty thoughtful of him to take that into consideration.

Next to the quietly sleeping Tillis, the two of us enjoy our mokemoke feast.

3

After a highly fulfilling evening, in more ways than one, it's now the next night.

With no skirmishes along the border recently, Rose and I, who don't have much use outside of combat, are wandering around among the festival stalls...

I find someone leaping over a line that shouldn't be crossed.

"Aww, how cute! A tiger!"

"Is there someone inside? Is it you, Grandpa?"

"I think it might be Misha's grandma."

A happily smiling Tiger Man is surrounded by three children.

The tiger mutant and proud lolicon appears to be masquerading as a stuffed animal for the festival.

"Rose, be ready. We encourage all sorts of villainy at Kisaragi, but touching children in a sexual way is an automatic death sentence. Russell's situation skirts the line because of his age. But that? That's way out-of-bounds. Rose, draw his attention from the front. He's an old comrade, so the least I can do is put him down myself."

"Boss, please calm down. The kids are clearly the ones approaching him, not the other way around."

Rose, who usually gets candy along with Russell, tries to plead Tiger Man's case.

But that's exactly what a predator wants.

The only good lolicon is one who stays far away from kids.

"Die, you damned pedophile!"

"Whaaat?! The hell is wrrrong with you, Six?!"

Realizing that Rose won't help me, I draw my R-Buzzsaw and slash at Tiger Man from behind.

But he's still a mutant, so his instincts are able to alert him to the attack.

"I'm sorry it's come to this, Tiger Man. I knew you were attracted to children, but I figured you were a gentleman. All pedos must die. That's an ironclad law of Kisaragi."

"What the hell are you talking about?! I haven't done anything! I'm an upstanding lolicon who's going to be modified into a little girl! Don't put lolicons and pedophiles on the same level!"

Tiger Man—no, Mr. Tiger Man—speaks with such conviction that he forgets to purr while speaking.

"I'm sorry, Mr. Tiger Man. My mistake. I suspected you for a moment because of all the vicious rumors claiming you became a mutant so you'd look like an animal plushie that kids would like. I'm sorry for doubting you."

"All is forrrgiven. Um… So who was saying that exactly? Lady Lilith should be the only one who knows that was the reason I became a mutant."

On second thought, maybe I should kill him right now.

Maybe I'll just put a strike on his record for now and wait.

"Tch, you scared all the kids away with your attack. I'm worrried about the kids, so I'll watch overrr the city from the shadows. My mutant senses tell me something might happen."

"It's fine for you to protect the brats, but could you avoid getting near them? For appearances' sake?"

As Rose and I watch Tiger Man leave, I hear something approaching at high speed.

Turning to face the sound, I see Grimm with a desperate expression on her face.

"THERRRRE YOU AAAARRRRE!"

Grimm shouts obnoxiously, sprinting in our direction.

"That was some stunt you pulled yesterday! It was awful! She was so intent on seducing me that I started to think maybe I'd be fine with a woman if she could make me happy. That was close!"

"Oh, you came all this way just to brag? Hey, Rose, that stall's food looks pretty good. Mind grabbing us some?"

"I always blow my salary on food whenever payday rolls around, so I'm broke. But we can still enjoy the smells."

The owner of the stall looks at a loss as we hang around to enjoy the appetizing aromas. Grimm takes out her wallet.

"Stop that; it's embarrassing. I'll buy you some! *Sigh...* Ever since the commander showed up, my precious wedding savings have been dwindling."

As Grimm sobs, I start munching on the grilled-meat skewer...

"Wow, Boss, look! It's the undead parade! The spirits that couldn't wait till the festival showed up early and wander around the city like that. Grimm made all those dolls."

"Pretty impressive, hmm? Not only am I a good seamstress, I'm pretty good at domestic chores in general."

At Rose's encouragement, Grimm starts singing her own praises.

"I'm impressed and all, but can't you make something other than stuffed animals for them to possess? I mean, aren't the spirits mostly old men and women?"

"Well sure, there tend to be a lot of older people, but watch what you say. There are plenty of young ghosts, too... Besides, it's kind of cute when your grandpa shows up as a stuffed animal."

It looks like there are only older spirits among the dolls assembled here.

The procession of human-size stuffed animals marches along in front of us—cute, except they're all possessed by the dead.

There are a few mischievous kids wandering among the dolls, following them around and occasionally kicking them.

Hey, that's that damned brat who keeps calling me the Fly!

I approach stealthily, hoping to pants him in public...

*   *   *

And suddenly, the dolls decide to dogpile me.

"Whoa! What the hell?! I haven't done anything to you! I was just gonna pants this kid!"

"Boss, why were you trying to do something so stupid? The spirits in the dolls are from this city. They could be related to that boy!" Rose shouts as the dolls assault me.

I could handle one or two, but there are way too many.

I resolve to absorb the blows and instead look for a chance to land a counter…

"Boss, this whole thing kind of makes me happy. Can we just stay like this for a bit?"

"Yeah, this is the first time I've felt at peace on this ruthless rock." I feel a warm tranquility at the center of this mob of stuffed animals. Even if they're ghosts on the inside, this is still pretty nice.

"Be careful, you two! There's something wrong here! The spirits are supposed to agree not to attack the living when they possess my dolls. But they're attacking the commander without any hesitation. Which means there might be a necromancer nearby…"

As the dolls surround the two of us, Grimm raises the alarm.

Honestly, getting attacked by these adorable things just feels like they're trying to play.

Just then, Grimm suddenly points her finger at the dolls. "I am Grimm, Archbishop of Lord Zenarith, the one who provided the bodies you currently possess. Cease your attacks at once. If not, I shall remove the blessings of undeath and send you back to Lord Zenarith…," she declares with a fierce look in her eyes.

"Don't, Grimm!" Rose warns. "If you're going to remove the blessing of undeath, you have to be really careful how you word it…"

Just as Rose starts her warning…

"O Great Lord Zenarith! Remove your blessing from the foolish undead assembled in this space!"

With her grand pronouncement, the dolls who had continued their attacks collapse in a heap at once.

And then—

"…Maybe we should just skip reviving her until the festival's over."

"…Well, I guess we have to gather more offerings…"

We spend a bit of time debating whether or not we should revive the foolish undead slumped in her wheelchair like a puppet with its strings cut.

4

Rose and I eventually decided to take Grimm to the cave. And so a day later…

"Six, you're just getting in my way. Make sure the wet clothes are stretched out nice and flat when you hang them up to dry, all right?"

"You're getting a little obsessive in your details. Don't let the fact that the others need you go to your head."

I'm in the temporary hideout at the park with Russell, hanging the washing out to dry. He's completely mastered the tasks required of a maid, establishing himself as a motherly figure to our Combat Agents. I suppose a former overlord in the Demon Lord's Army would pick this stuff up quickly.

"Hey, Russell, I heard we're having curry for dinner. Make sure it's heavy on the meat, and skip the carrots and potatoes, all right? Onions are fine."

"Don't be ridiculous! No picky eating allowed. Oh, and make sure you wash your own underwear. If you put them in the basket once you're done, I'll make sure to dry them."

He's completely adapted to his role.

I suppose it might be because Chimeras are quick to adjust to their environment.

After I finish washing my underwear, Russell tells me to go out and play until dinnertime, so I grab the bored-looking Alice and wander around town.

"Hey, Six, there's an unusual-looking stall there. Go check it out."

After curiously surveying the surroundings, Alice points to a place that sells skewers: the most common sort of outdoor food stall.

Where there's a festival, there's food vendors. And where there's food vendors, there's a golden opportunity for Kisaragi.

"That's a grilled-skewer stall, all right; leave it to me... Yo, yo, yo, just who gave you permission to put a shop out here? Hand over one of those skewers, dammit!"

"I already have permission from the health inspectors and the country...," the owner of the stall babbles as he hands over a skewer.

I have Alice pay for the skewer and take a bite.

"Hmph! Just what sort of meat is this? I can't say I've had it before. You're not using any shady ingredients, are you?"

I open with a complaint in lieu of a greeting. The idea is to threaten to spread bad rumors if the owner doesn't comply with our demands.

"......I-it's perfectly...normal?" The owner cowers at my threat, refusing to meet my gaze...

"...Now wait just a damned minute. What is this meat? There's nothing about what this is. Just what are you using?"

"O-orc meat, of course! Completely normal orc meat! We run a perfectly clean operation here! If you plan to disrupt our business, we might...not call the guards... But at least we'll make a fuss with the crowds... No, dammit, that'd be a problem, too..."

......

"What'd you just say, old man? You're serving illegal meat you can't have the guards knowing about, aren't you?!" I drop my act and corner the owner, who's in a genuine panic, but he still refuses to meet my gaze.

"Hey, Six. I can't identify this meat visually."

"Meat that Alice can't identify?! That's really messed up! Don't move. I'm getting the guards!"

"W-wait, please! All right, all right, I understand. You're quite the villain, my friend. I'll happily give you five free skewers. So please don't go around spreading rumors…"

He looks over at me with a shady smile, skewers in hand, but still won't say what his meat came from.

What the hell did I just eat?

"This is definitely not a shop we can leave open! Come along; I'm handing you over to the guards!"

"You got me! You got me! Have seven, no, eight skewers! Hell, I'll give you ten if you'll just…"

Just as I'm about to take the owner into custody…

"What are you doing…?"

…Snow is suddenly standing there with an exasperated look on her face.

"Oh! Hey, debt girl, good timing. This old man's selling some really odd mystery meat. You're supposed to be a knight, right? Take him away."

"W-wait, I'm not selling anything illegal! It's just a little unusual…"

At our exchange, Snow peers in closely at the skewers, and…

"Eh?! Wh-why are you selling this…? Well, it's not illegal. Technically, it's not illegal, but…"

Just what the hell is this stuff?!

…As Snow looks at the owner with shock, he presses something into her hand.

"Lady Knight, this is just a sign of my appreciation. We wouldn't be able to prepare for the Undead Festival so peacefully if not for your efforts, after all…"

"I-indeed? Y-yes, of course. But this meat… Well, I suppose it's not poisonous, and what people don't know can't hurt them."

"That's right; it's just meat! Ha-ha-ha-ha-ha."

Snow happily pockets the bribe, and the owner laughs with relief.

I point to the pair as Alice brings over someone from a local guard station.

"Officer, those are the perps!"

5

"Tch, I missed out on a chance to make some money, thanks to you. If you're going to interrupt my side gig, I've got some methods of my own, you know."

"This sounds weird coming from me, but that's not a harmless side gig, and you know it."

She's been in a foul mood since she was forced to return the bribe to the stall owner who had to close up shop after getting a lecture from the guards.

Given how shocked the guard looked after examining the meat, I really want to know what the hell it was.

"Fool. If I actually see illegal activity while on patrol, I'll arrest the perpetrators. There's nothing wrong with overlooking some legally gray activities during the festival, but that freedom can go to their heads. So sometimes you need to set an example."

"You had tears in your eyes when you had to give back that bribe. And you spent so long bitching at the guard."

"S-silence!" Snow retorts. "I need to earn money so I can pay back Lady Alice as quickly as possible. You should let me know if you think of any good business opportunities. If it makes a profit, I'll give you your share."

I seriously consider telling her about my boob-shaped pudding idea, but she's still technically one of my soldiers, so I don't want to see her fall quite that far.

Though I suppose it's already too late for that...

As I look at Snow like a disappointed parent, Alice tugs on my sleeve. "Forget about that for a moment, Six. We should try attacking one of those dolls. Grimm claims they've got ghosts inside, right? I don't know what sort of scam she's running, but we should use the power of science to expose it."

"You really do hate fantasy elements, don't you? The spirits in those things are former residents of the city, right? We'll get in trouble if we hurt them."

Snow shoots us a look of distaste upon hearing our exchange.

"What are you two planning? Even if it's for Lady Alice, I'd prefer not to disrupt the festival welcoming back the dead..."

Just then...

...an oddly sprightly stuffed animal surveys its surroundings in front of us.

The pink rabbit starts making its way toward the park where we've set up our temporary hideout. Something's fishy here.

We decide to follow it.

The stuffed rabbit arrives at the park without noticing us. After ducking into the bushes, it begins studying our hideout intently...

...and falls over as Alice unleashes a sneak attack from behind.

"Six, I've caught one behaving suspiciously. Let's see what's inside."

"Good work, Alice! Hang on a moment; I'll tie it up with some rope... Huh, we've got a lively one here. Hey, cut it out!"

"—! —!!"

I hear a muffled voice from inside the doll; does that mean ghosts have vocal cords?

Alice keeps it pinned while I start wrapping the rope around it, but the thing is really struggling.

"H-hey, you two! The spirit inside died for Grace! Treat it with a little more respect…" Snow steps in to stop us, but this rabbit's resisting harder than I expected.

"This thing's pretty strong for a ghost! Alice, go ahead and show it who's boss. Use it as a sandbag, and…"

As I tie up the doll and instruct Alice, I feel something soft to the touch.

For some reason, the doll ignores the kicks Alice is landing on it and instead resists my attempts to grab it.

Did Grimm make this stuffed rabbit?

It's pretty comfortable to hold, almost enough to want one in every home.

<Evil Points Acquired. Evil Points Acquired.>

For some reason, I get points each time I touch the doll.

Just as I start fondling various parts of the doll because of the pleasant sensations…

"…! …!! S-stop already!"

The rabbit lets out a cry and stands up, emitting flame from its palm.

I wonder for a moment if ghosts can use magic, but the voice sounds familiar.

"Getting pretty handsy, aren't you? You bastard, I'm going to finish you off once and for—!"

The rabbit starts to speak, but the flame forming in the palm of its hand sets its torso on fire.

"…! …!! …!!!"

Suddenly bursting into flames, the rabbit rolls around the ground trying to put out the fire.

It looks like it's got a good bit of fire resistance.

Roughly splitting open the rabbit suit, what emerges from inside is—

"*Gasp, wheeze…!* L-long time no see, Six! I'm impressed you saw through my disguise!"

Tanned skin, generous curves.

A skimpy outfit like a swimsuit that just barely covers enough skin.

"I—I wasn't expecting you to blow my cover in the middle of this city, but now that you have, I have no choice. Come on, Six; let's get started…!"

Heine of the Flames babbles quickly, as though to distract from the fact that she almost died from her own power. She makes for an easy mark and is captured without much effort.

6

In front of the Grace city park…

Heine is lying on the grass a little distance away from our hideout, her upper body bound with rope and her eyes filled with tears.

"Wasn't expecting to find Heine inside one of those. Hey, Alice, the stuffed animal *gacha* just gave us an SSR result."

"A stuffed animal *gacha*? Really? Still, we've proven that the dolls wandering around town have people inside. There's no such thing as ghosts, after all."

As we're debating, Snow bends down in front of Heine with a wide grin on her face.

"Ha-ha-ha-ha-ha-ha! To think one of the Demon Lord's Elite Four would be in a place like this! What, were you that eager to become my bonus pay? I simply adore the sight of you helpless and tied up on the ground like that!"

The deeply disturbed sadist looks down at Heine and cackles.

Heine's eyes are still welling with tears, but she purses her lips and glares up in defiance.

"Bwa-ha-ha-ha. We've got plenty of time. I'll enjoy getting your reasons for sneaking into this city out of you... Mwa-ha-ha... mwa-ha-ha-ha!"

I don't know what she's thinking of doing, but Snow shivers with a blissful expression on her face, wrapping her arms around herself.

"Wait. I'll handle Heine's interrogation. Go wait over there and stay out of my way."

I push aside the wriggling Snow and step out in front.

The moment Heine sees me, she goes pale.

"Wha—? Nonsense! You expect me to give up a chance to look down on this stubborn woman and torture her?! I bet you want to just indulge in your perversions. I'll handle this!"

"Don't be ridiculous. We've captured a female enemy commander dressed like this! Not doing a perverted interrogation would go against the laws of nature!"

Ignoring our bickering, Alice takes out a syringe and bends down.

"Why bother with interrogating? Leave this to me. I'll draw out the information by dosing her with a powerful truth serum. If that doesn't work, I'll mess directly with her brain using surgery."

"Eeep...!" Heine squeaks out a cry at Alice's idea.

"Hey, Alice, that's the human vegetable course. That'd be a waste. Heh-heh, are you ready, Miss Heine? There aren't too many reasons why someone would sneak into a city. You're here for sabotage, aren't you?"

"Wait, we should let her decide what she prefers! Choose, Heine of the Flames. Pain, perversion, or become a vegetable?"

Heine, now completely pale, looks up at us from her bonds.

"I-I'm just here to rescue Russell! I figured I could hide among the wandering stuffed animals... I'm not here to sabotage you..."

I grab a handful of Heine's breast as she pleads tearfully.

"Don't lie! I bet you guys are behind all the setbacks we've had during our base construction!"

"N-no, no, no, I don't know anything about that! I sent some orcs to raid along your border to get you to focus in that direction, but I don't know anything about your base!"

As I hear the announcements of Evil Point acquisition, I put my compassion aside and continue groping Heine to get her to spill the rest of her information.

"Ah-ha, so you must be the reason I've lost my beloved blades and fallen heavily into debt! How dare you! I'll demand a ransom for your safe return to the Demon Lord's Army!"

"Wh-what are you talking about?! I don't know anything about your debts! Don't blame everything on me! Six, I really am only here to get Russell back! You can stop groping me now... Hell, I'm pretty sure you're just using interrogating me as an excuse to grope me!"

I suppose I should have expected this from one of the Demon Lord's Elite Four.

She won't spill her real reasons for being here so easily...

"S-stop, th-that's not funny! Don't try to strip me here!"

Heine desperately struggles to crawl away, but that act won't work on me.

I'm tugging on the fabric that's just barely covering Heine's assets when Alice raises her hand to stop me.

"I think that's enough, Six. It looks like she really is just here to recover Russell of the Water."

It's not often Alice says something like that. There's no way she'd be swayed by pity, so I bet she's got some reason for butting in.

"Tch. If Alice believes you, then we'll let you go for today."

"You're in luck, Heine of the Flames! You better appreciate Lady Alice's mercy!"

I'm just putting on an act, but Snow genuinely sounds like Alice's lackey.

"Th-thanks, I appreciate it… Anyway, do you mind letting me see Russell? He's powerful, but he's still just a kid. Please don't do anything too awful to him…"

"Doesn't matter if he's a kid or not, he's still technically a leader in an evil organization. We're not treating him too badly, though. See for yourself," I tell her.

Heine breathes a small sigh of relief, then stands while tied up.

"Russell's over there; go ahead and talk to him. He's working, but I'm sure he can spare the time to chat."

"All right. I really appreciate it! Russell! Russell, it's me! Are you all right? How are you doing? You haven't been mistreated, right?"

Encouraged by Alice, Heine looks toward the temporary hideout where the cross-dressing Chimera is busily hanging up the laundry to dry and freezes in her tracks.

Russell, happily humming a song as he hangs up the washing, twitches at the call from his former coworker.

"H-Heine…? Huh, wh-what are you doing here, Heine…?!"

"…R-Russell…? Wh-wh-what are you doing dressed like that…?"

Of course, "like that" refers to the maid outfit.

Recently, the cross-dressing Chimera has settled into his role and seems to be enjoying caring for Tiger Man and the Combat Agents.

"Russell, y-you…"

"N-no, this is… Heine, this isn't what it looks like! They're just forcing me to dress this way! It's Tiger Man's fetish!" Russell desperately pleads his case as Heine backs away, but the fact that he was humming earlier robs him of credibility.

Alice pats Heine's shoulder as she stands there staring in shock. "As you can see, Russell's leading a fulfilling life here. Seems he enjoys caring for the others instead of being judged solely for his fighting ability like he was in the Demon Lord's Army. Put aside any ideas of taking him back to the Demon Lord's Army and just let him be."

"You're right; I've never seen Russell so cheerful... Honestly, Russell, it hurts to lose you, but... You're still a kid. It's better for you to live each day happily instead of going to war. Enjoy your life here..."

"Hey, wait! Heine, don't leave me here! I mean, sure, I'll admit the work is a little fun, and I was happy when they said they needed me! But I want to go back to the Demon Lord's Army, I swear!"

Heine looks like she's seriously thinking it through as Russell clings to her.

"...I think sticking to a peaceful life here is a valid choice... But it's also true that we need you," Heine says with a little smirk. "Alice, right? You seem to be the voice of reason around here... How about we make a deal?"

"Not happening. You don't seem to understand your position, you airheaded floozy."

Heine freezes at Alice's harsh response.

"All right, Six, we're done here. This woman's now your maid for generating Evil Points. Do whatever you'd like, including sexual harassment. Make her earn her keep."

"Whoo-hoo!"

"Wait! I'm sorry I mentioned a deal! But I have important information for you!" Heine pleads desperately as I crack my knuckles and approach.

"Do you have mush for brains? Given the circumstances, we can force you to spill whatever information you might hold. I'll send Six to you, so you can start talking whenever you're ready."

"All right! Feeling motivated now!"

"I'll talk! I'll talk! The information is about the Undead Festival that starts tomorrow! The undead have been acting odd lately, right? There's a reason for that!"

My gleeful hands pause at Heine's words.

Oh yeah, Grimm was saying something similar.

Stuff about zombies staying hostile and the dolls attacking people.

But as I try to press for details…

"You're going on about superstitious nonsense like the undead, too? We're done. You're not even worth being a maid. I'm going to just hog-tie you and toss you out into the wastes!"

"Whaaat?! What do you mean, 'superstitious nonsense'?! It's about the undead! If you hold the festival now, you'll face some serious trouble!"

"We're an evil organization. Causing trouble is how we put food on the table. Bringing chaos to the world is my job. Bring it on. Six, go toss her outside the city."

Alice ignores Heine's words and hands the rope's end to me.

"You sure? I bet she's still got plenty of uses."

"That's right. If we negotiate with the Demon Lord's Army, we can definitely turn a profit with this woman. It'd be a waste to just leave her to the monsters!"

Despite our pleading…

"Negotiations are a pain. Just go and throw her away. We'll show them we're the greater evil organization. She'll set a perfect example as mokemoke fodder," Alice says, shoving our objections aside.

"All right, we left Heine in the wastes. She was crying and causing a scene. Are you sure we should've just left her like that?"

"Good work. It's fine. She's plenty useful this way."

…Useful? How?

"Even one of the Demon Lord's Elite Four won't come away unscathed if you leave them tied up in a wasteland."

"Don't worry about that. I made sure the knots were in a place where she could burn them away. And I made sure they were loosely tied so she could undo them even without her flames. She'll figure out how to free herself once she calms down a bit."

Um.

"Then we just wait for her to return to the Demon Lord's castle, and we'll know the location, thanks to the tracking device I put on her. We could have just interrogated the intel out of her, but they'll be less cautious if she returns on her own. Once we know the location, we can launch an attack on them."

………

"Um, Alice. Right before we ditched Heine, I took away the magic stone she had hidden away. Also, I noticed the knots were loose, so I made sure to tighten them…"

"Seriously?"

………

"Oh well. She's one of the Demon Lord's Elite Four. She's not that easy to kill."

"O-of course. She's an elite. She'll be fine."

"J-just like that? Really…?"

7

The next day.

"Hey, Six, what happened to Heine? She better be safe."

Russell's been pestering me ever since we ditched Heine in the wastes.

"You're our prisoner. You've got plenty to worry about yourself. I've got a plan brewing. We'll make a maid café and have you work there. Once the guests are comfortable, we'll reveal that you're actually a man. That'll earn us lots of money and Evil Points. A lovely plan, isn't it?"

"I still think you lot are more evil than the Demon Lord's Army."

As Russell and I continue washing underwear in the park fountain, Alice calls over to us.

"Hey, Six, sorry to interrupt you as you're getting used to homeless life, but I need you to come with me. I'm meeting the princess."

Oh.

"Ah, so we're going to force them to open up the barracks and free us from this life," I say. "Tents are just too drafty. Let's have them give us the room I had before."

"Thanks to the antics of you Combat Agents, we're not allowed in the castle unless we're on urgent business," Alice retorts. "And that's precisely what we're going for today."

I tilt my head. "Didn't they say they'd let us get away with some minor evil deeds? As long as we avoid crossing certain lines like hurting people or committing seriously unspeakable acts."

"Correct. We've had them ignore petty crimes as part of the cost of protecting this kingdom. Which means…"

Alice lets out an oddly human sigh.

"…some idiot crossed a line and got caught," she says with a look of resignation.

The moment we enter the castle, we're taken to Tillis's room with no explanation.

There, the room's owner sits with an expression that's difficult to read.

"…Sir Six, Miss Alice. Given that we've built up a good relationship, I must express my supreme disappointment over this incident," she murmurs. The scheming princess seems to be having trouble telling us what she wants to say.

I'm still not sure why we're here, but she doesn't seem too angry.

Alice usually takes charge when problems like this come up, and this time is no different. "Sorry about all this, princess. I've been keeping a close eye on these meatheads, but… First, can you tell me what's going on? We can discuss reparations and other issues after."

"Certainly. For reparations, a monetary payment will not be necessary. The attempt ended in failure. As for the crime… Shall we call it an attempt to sneak in and seduce a sleeping maiden? The victim in this case…is myself."

Alice's capacity for smooth talk seems to leave her.

"...Seriously?! We have a Combat Agent who's got the balls to attempt that on the princess? Huh," she mutters in shock, which is impressive for an android.

Tillis turns a pained expression toward her. "The one who made the attempt is Agent Ten. He's currently being detained in the castle dungeon."

Wait, Agent Ten?

That's odd. He's definitely a first-class pervert, but he's also a gentleman.

I can't imagine him making the moves on Tillis while she sleeps...

As though answering my doubts, Tillis speaks a little more clearly, a faint blush creeping into her cheeks.

"Unlike the other Kisaragi agents, Agent Ten had a good reputation within the castle, and he was well-known for his generosity to children, which makes his attempt at nighttime seduction of royalty all the more...disappointing...," Tillis trails off, seeming especially shocked by this turn of events. Agent Ten the gentleman is indeed quite popular among the children.

"I had no idea he was that much of an evil bastard... Wow..."

During this whole exchange, only Alice seems to be impressed.

"What do you mean, 'wow'?! I woke up in the middle of the night to find a completely naked Agent Ten hunched over near me. Do you have any idea how frightening that was...?!"

"All right, understood. We'll go ahead and grill him about the details. Just to confirm, it was only an attempt, right? Can you elaborate on how far he got...?"

When Alice asks for further details, Tillis clutches her arms around herself and trembles as if remembering that moment.

I'm also curious about just what he did to Tillis, but now's not the time.

As the two of them are busy discussing the next steps to take, I head to the dungeon where Ten's likely being held.

8

Returning to the room a bit later, I find the two of them still going at it.

"As I said, there's no need for monetary compensation. So we would require some other form of recompense. Sharing some of Kisaragi's technology, for example..."

"Now you're just being greedy, princess. I'm skeptical on whether or not your body even has the same value as our tech. For example, if you're not a virgin, the value would be substantially less—"

"There's no way a royal princess would be that indecent! I haven't yet—"

"Sorry to interrupt during such an interesting subject, but can you spare a moment?"

I interject myself into the apparent argument.

"I spoke to Ten to see what he was up to, and he says he wasn't there to seduce the princess. He says the reason he was naked in Tillis's room was because he was trying to poop here."

"......?!?!?!?!?!?! Excuse me—I'm afraid I don't understand. I don't understand a word of what you're saying!" cries Tillis with a rare show of confusion.

"...? Oh, he says he was naked because he can't relax in a room with his clothes on. I've met people like that before."

"No, that's not what I meant! Well, all right, that's also a serious issue, but still! No, what I wanted to know was why he was planning to do such a thing inside my room! Why wouldn't he just go to the bathroom?!"

It's rare to see Tillis so flustered.

"I don't know, either. Guess he's just marking his territory? Setting boundaries?"

"My bedroom is my own! Honestly...?! J-just...just give me a moment to gather my thoughts...," Tillis says, looking as incredulous as ever; but after pressing her hand to her chest and taking several deep breaths, her expression returns to normal. "I admit, I would have found this easier to accept if it had been a seduction attempt... P-pardon me, but I must ask, in your country, is it common to sneak into a woman's room and do such things, Sir Six...?"

"Of course not, don't be ridiculous. You feeling okay?"

"I—I find that abnormal as well. I was only asking just in case! Of all the... What crime do I even charge him with...?!"

Just then, Alice—who had been frozen until that moment for some reason—returns to her senses and reboots.

"Hey, Six, seems like I still have a lot to learn. I thought I understood you Combat Agents, but there are times when I can't make heads or tails of what you're thinking."

Well, of course, even a high-spec android isn't perfect.

"That's how it is sometimes. I mean, it hasn't been that long since you were built. You just need to build up experience from here. Everyone starts somewhere."

"...If you say so. I don't feel like I'll ever understand you all, but..."

"Have a little more faith in yourself. It'll be all right. You've been doing really well already."

Alice doesn't seem convinced. She's got a wide range of expressions for an android.

But anyway.

"So what's going to happen with Ten? Since we can't expect reinforcements from Earth, Combat Agents are a precious commodity. Losing him would put a wrench in our future operations..."

"Hmm?! O-oh, of course; what shall we do...? Given the lack of precedent, I'm not certain what offense this would fall under..."

Tillis seems at a loss, so I offer her a hand.

"It's not much different from peeing in public. So a similar punishment should be enough."

"Please don't equate using a maiden's bedroom as a toilet with something like peeing in public!"

Tillis turns red, as if realizing something after her outburst.

"…You know, you're still a girl, even if you are a scheming royal… You probably shouldn't be yelling out things like 'peeing in public'…"

"Whose fault do you think that is?! …This is too much! First the idiotic incantation, and now men breaking into my bedroom…"

Tillis suddenly cradles her face and bursts into tears. I guess it's stressful to shoulder all the responsibility for running the kingdom.

"Alice, if you've got a heart in your robotic chest, at least try to console her…"

"…I do sympathize with her. If I were her, I would just kick all the Combat Agents out."

Tillis purses her lips and glares at us. "We'll write this incident off as a minor infraction this time. But if anything like this happens in the future, we'll take strict measures. What is our security even doing…?"

Tillis seems at a loss, so I decide to offer her some advice here as well.

"The security for this room sucks. The problem is there's only one soldier watching the doorway and no one watching the ceiling. I've lost count of how many times I've sneaked into this room."

"?!" Tillis goes quiet and stares in shock.

Yes, during my infiltration missions of late, I'd driven climbing stakes into the castle wall and opened a hole in the roof to sneak in.

Recently, taking advantage of a time when Tillis wasn't in the room and there was no one around, I'd done a little work to make part of the ceiling easier to remove for access.

"See, like this…"

"So you were the root cause! Which means Sir Six was sneaking in to seduce me…" Tillis hugs her arms to herself and looks at me as though I'm some sort of predator.

"No, that thought never occurred to me. It's just that I can earn a ton of Evil Points just by sneaking into a royal's room. At first, I was planning to sneak in, strip naked, and crawl into bed next to you while you were sleeping, then surprise you when you woke up. But since I found out I could earn a lot of points just from sneaking in, I figured it'd be better to use the place to rack them up without your knowledge."

"What do you mean 'you figured'?! Huh? W-wait a moment; the way you phrased that sounds like it wasn't just you and Ten sneaking in…"

Tillis's expression goes from shock to dread.

"The others were here, too. Every night, there's been someone here earning points by doing push-ups, dancing, or whatever else next to you."

"Wh-why?! Just what were you doing while I slept?! And *why*?!"

As to why it turned out that way, I really don't know, either.

"It started out with my squats. I'd sneak in during the middle of the night, get some exercise in, then head home to sleep. After that, there was the time I snuck in and played Jenga next to you. It started getting exciting to see how long it would take you to notice, and it was also fun to test the limits of what we could get away with. Recently, we actually had a barbecue right next to you…"

Before I can finish, Tillis screams an order.

"Guards!!"

"Concerning Multigenic Life-Forms, Code-Named: Chimeras"

Six, have you been doing well?

Every day is filled with intense fighting here on Earth.

According to Alice's reports, things seem pretty rough over there as well. But I hope

you will return as soon as possible.

The samples from your planet are all very fascinating.

The creatures don't make any evolutionary sense or have signs of gene editing.

But since you're a meathead, it probably won't do much good for me to take the time

to explain this to you tactfully and politely.

Anyway, I'll leave out the details, but concerning the girl you call a Chimera, just bear

in mind that there's no way that something like her could have evolved naturally on

that planet.

I've gone ahead and written an academic paper on the subject. Please have a look at

it sometime if you'd like.

I know you mentioned getting sleepy when reading more than three lines at a time,

so have Alice give you a summary.

Regardless, I'm glad to hear you're doing fine over there.

Astaroth and Belial both look a little unfulfilled every day, as though

something's missing.

I have to admit I'm also looking forward to a speedy return for you,

so take care of yourself...

Lilith

1

"Sheesh, I was just trying to give her advice on security. No need to get so angry."

"I honestly think you should be glad she didn't press charges because you weren't caught in the act…"

I guess Ten's gonna be locked up for a while longer. Right when we need all hands on deck for base construction, too.

As a result, we've decided to delay the construction of the hideout until he gets released.

With nothing to do, Alice and I are wandering around the city of Grace and looking for opportunities to earn Evil Points.

"So I guess that's how you were earning the points to order the construction materials and equipment. Hey, Six, sneak into the king's room next."

"No way; why would I want to sneak into some old man's room? The fun is in sneaking in and doing stuff next to a defenseless beautiful maiden without waking her. But rest assured, the unwritten rule was to avoid laying a finger on Tillis."

"What is it with you and your unwritten rules? If you're going to go through all the trouble, at least have the balls to make a move on her."

I wish someone who looks like a pretty young girl wouldn't say stuff like that.

"Anyway, Six, why don't we set fire to those wandering dolls?"

"Given how normal you are, you really do lose your head when the supernatural gets involved."

There's a good reason Alice is making such dangerous suggestions.

After all that preparation, the Undead Festival is finally underway, and tons of stuffed animals are wandering around every part of the city.

Given her utter refusal to believe in fantasy worlds, the situation's gotta be unbearable for her.

"I eventually plan to expose the scam behind Grimm's curses as well. They're all just some sort of hypnosis."

"Don't say that to Grimm; you'll just start another fight."

At that moment, we catch sight of something in front of us.

"…Hey, Six. Isn't that Grimm?"

Yes, speaking of the devil, there's Grimm in the middle of a gathering of people.

"Lady Grimm, what is my brother saying? Um, is my brother really in here…?"

A shy-looking young woman pleads to Grimm tearfully.

She looks to be about fourteen or fifteen years old.

Grimm smiles warmly at her, then gently presses the doll next to her.

"I'm not certain if he is your brother, but his name is Larius. He says, 'I'm home. I'm glad you achieved your dream without me. I'm so proud of you. I was so worried you wouldn't be able to get by on your own, but I'm reassured to see you doing so well.'"

"Larius!"

Overcome with emotion, the girl hugs the stuffed animal.

"I—I worked so hard! Even after Mom, Dad, and then you died… I kept at it all by myself!"

The stuffed animal gently wraps its arms around the girl.

"He says, 'It must have been so hard for you. I'm so proud of you, Mariel. I'm so very proud of you, Little Sister.'"

"Bwaaaaaah!" The girl called Mariel bursts into tears, clinging to the stuffed animal.

The people watching the exchange also have tears in their eyes.

I find myself pleasantly surprised to see this new side of Grimm.

"'When my shy and fragile sister Mariel said she wanted to become a brawler and hold both gold and glory in the palms of her hands, I wanted to stop you. I thought you'd taken leave of your senses… But I'm happy to admit I was wrong. You've worked so hard to get where you are.'"

"Yup! Um, um…! I haven't lost a single match yet, and my fans even call me 'Bloody Mary'! And now, the champion, Reidog, keeps finding excuses to avoid fighting me…"

…

Wait, is this really a heartwarming story?

I mean, the crowd is nodding along tearfully, but I'm not sure her brother was wrong to stop her.

"Hey, Larius, what happened to Mom and Dad?"

"'Oh, those two were reincarnated a while ago. They were fighting till the end, declaring to the other they were going to find a better partner and avoid a shotgun wedding in the next life.'"

"Oh, Mom and Dad… Heh, how funny… Still fighting even after death, heh-heh…," Mariel chuckles softly.

Nope, that's not the least bit heartwarming.

C'mon, guys; stop laughing along and point that out.

"Now go on home and enjoy the rest of the festival. He should be able to communicate through writing, though it might be a little hard to read since he'll be writing with a doll's hand."

"Thank you very much, Lady Grimm! Let's go home, Larius! When we get home, I'll show you my Skull Crusher, the move that earned me the nickname 'Bloody Mary'!" Mariel smiles and takes the doll by the hand, and the two walk off, arm in arm.

"Lady Grimm, me next! Please, me next!"

"I'm certain my husband is in here! Lady Grimm, please tell me what my husband says!"

After Mariel leaves, the members of the crowd begin pleading for Grimm's attention.

"Please, all of you, calm down. We'll go in order... Also, you there. Your husband is no longer here. He's already been reincarnated, but he said something about marrying a young, cute bride in his next— Ow! H-hey, stop that!" Grimm cries out as the doll starts hitting her in the middle of her story. "Sorry, sorry, I was only kidding! But can I just point out that it's completely unfair for you to flirt with your wife through me?!"

Makes me think it'd be better not to let her run this festival, but I guess since she's the only one who can talk to the spirits, there's not much of an alternative.

We turn away from the sight of Grimm interpreting between the spirits and their bereaved families, resuming our wandering around the festival.

"That was a rare sight, to see her acting all priestly. Pretty impressive, talking to the dead."

As we wander around the city, I think back on how different my impression of Grimm was tonight.

"Try not to buy into her bullshit, would you, Six? There's a perfectly reasonable explanation for what we saw earlier. That Mariel, or whatever her name was, was a plant. She and Grimm must have planned it beforehand and put on an act."

"You really hate fantasy, don't you?"

I have trouble believing that girl's tearful expression was just an act.

I look over the stuffed animals as they walk past.

"It's certainly a cutesy little scene. Grimm's supposedly the one who made all those dolls wandering around. She's got a pretty domestic streak, it seems."

Well, considering how badly she wants to get married, it shouldn't be all that surprising.

Walking next to me, Alice eyes the dolls as well. "Our Meat the Ripper is cuter."

"You and Rose have weird taste."

I take another look around the city. "So, Alice, this is what passes for a festival on this planet, I guess. What do you think?"

"No drama, no shady con artists. This planet's festivals are rather orderly, aren't they?"

For an evil organization like Kisaragi, festivals are how we got our start, and they remain an important part of our heritage.

Back when we were still small and weak, we'd put up unauthorized stalls whenever there was a festival to earn money.

Of course, that would lead to skirmishes with the local organizations, which we'd use to secure a foothold and…

"This really takes me back… I remember when I'd sell fake copies of rare cards from that super-popular trading card game to the kids…"

"Ripping off kids. Yikes."

Still…

"Anyway, as Kisaragi operatives, we can't just stand by and watch such a lame festival. Festivals mean fighting and scams. Hey, Alice, let's go show the locals what a real festival looks like."

Alice looks at me and tilts her head.

2

"Hey, you there! We've got boobies here! Big boobies! Whaddaya think? We're doin' a four-for-one boob deal if you act now!"

"Huh? Wh-what are you talking about?"

This is the city's hospitality district. Using money borrowed from Alice, we've rented a small space for the festival.

"C'mon, bro, you know what I'm talkin' about! Boobies, of course! They're soft, warm, and make you happy just by lookin' at 'em! Everyone loves boobies!"

"Everyone loves…"

"Boobies, yes."

There aren't any hostess clubs in this town. There are more direct forms of prostitution like brothels, but perhaps there just isn't much demand for bars where men can drink surrounded by beautiful women. After all, this country has way more women than men.

I smile at the customer, rubbing my hands together.

"For just five silver pieces an hour, you can spend time with some pretty young women. How about it? Refresh yourself with tasty booze and bountiful boobies."

"I'm in."

Seems this guy doesn't have much resistance to this sort of thing, as he accepts the invitation quite readily.

I show him inside before he changes his mind.

"You're in luck today! Right now, our number one hostess, Miss Snow, is available! Customer incoming!"

In the dimly lit interior, Snow awaits him on a sofa, wearing a dress that really shows off the goods.

"Welcome! I'm this club's number one hostess, Snow. Why don't we start things off with some drinks?"

"H-huh? D-drinks? Sure, do what you want…"

"Oh my, thank you very much! Boss, an order for drinks!"

The Number One asks for drinks without so much as an explanation of how customers are charged.

The man sits next to the Number One without the faintest notion of what sort of establishment this is. Then, without giving him any time to think, the club's Number Two brings a bottle and some glasses over and places them on the table.

"I brought the drinks. Here ya go."

Number Two is Alice, wearing a dress that shows off her shoulders.

Obviously, since this club's only got two hostesses, she ends up being the Number Two by default.

"Apologies, sir. Alice's mouthiness is part of her charm. Now drink up. Since you're the only customer, we'll go ahead and give you a deal and have two girls entertain you."

"O-oh, thanks… But didn't you say earlier there'd be four boobs? There are only two boobs in this club, as far as I can see…"

The man appears to remember what I told him up front.

He takes a long look at Snow's chest, then glances toward Alice, looking less than satisfied.

"Eh? What is it? You trying to start a fight with Kisaragi? This is the optimal size for high-spec functionality. You got it?"

"I'm not trying to tell you anything. Also, I don't understand what you're saying."

As Alice squabbles with him, Snow wastes no time and pours the man a drink.

"There you are, sir. Please have a drink."

Having already serviced two prior customers, Snow seems to have gotten a handle on how to deal with our current guest. Meanwhile, Alice continues to entertain the man with an attitude that veers between threatening and encouraging.

The man continues to cast glances at Snow's chest, but he doesn't appear to have the courage to get handsy, instead making small talk as they encourage him to buy more drinks.

After an hour quickly passes by, I sidle up to the table as planned.

"Enjoying your time here, sir? Your hour is almost up. Would you like an extension?"

"Huh? It's already been an hour? Well, five silvers for this much booze is a steal! All right, I'll take another hour or so..." The man laughs cheerfully, taking out the silver coins.

"Oh, don't be silly, sir. The five silver pieces are just to cover *your* drinks. Miss Snow's drinks, the hostess fees for two girls, and the potato chips add up to twenty gold pieces..."

"Whoa! I don't have that much money! Hey, that wasn't the deal!" The man starts to panic.

Festivals are a scam city.

That's right; we're taking advantage of the festival to run a rip-off hostess club to earn both Evil Points and invasion funds. Having lost our ability to earn points using Tillis's bedroom, we've had to find an alternate source to get by.

"You know, I did give Miss Snow permission to get one drink at first, but the rest were things she ordered on her own..."

"Is that true, Miss Snow?"

"I dunno."

As Snow plays up the part of a bimbo, the man's face contorts with fear.

"Hmph! Miss Snow says she doesn't know! Also, you sexually harassed Miss Alice for being flat! We'll be charging you recompense for that, too!"

<Evil Points Acquired>

"Mm-hmm, that really traumatized me. I'll settle for ten gold pieces."

<Evil Points Acquired>

"But she's just a kid! She's clearly got no boobs!"

<Evil Points Acquired>

As the man tries to put up some resistance, Alice and I stand up.

"Well, that's a problem, sir. If you have no money, we'll need to have you show us to your home."

<Evil Points Acquired>

"I've got a pretty good eye for things. I'll start by appraising your belongings."

<Evil Points—>

"That's enough, announcer!"

As I bitch at my internal announcements, the man finally loses it.

"Screw you! I can't believe you're running a scam like this! If I'm gonna pay that much money, I'm gonna grope Miss Snow's boobs!"

"Wh-what?! Don't be ridiculous! Have you lost your mind? Hey, Six, Alice, stop him! I'm not going to let him touch me for so little!"

Feeling he's got nothing left to lose, the man pounces on Snow to get his money's worth, but there's no way a knight like Snow would lose to a civilian.

Yet, lust proves itself a powerful motivator. Now grappling with Snow, the man is actually holding his own against her.

"Good work, Snow! Let's make this a fait accompli!"

"Yep, once that happens, we can get our share even if it goes to court. Well done, Number One. You're in rare form today."

"Stop commenting and stop him! …Grrr, this man's putting up stiff resistance for a commoner…!"

As the nondescript man puts up a good fight, the door suddenly bursts open.

"Freeze! City guard! We've received reports that you're running an illegal business here…"

Before the guards who burst in can finish, Alice and I break for the back door.

"W-wait, at least let me recover the money..." Snow hurriedly swats the man she's grappling with aside and grabs the club's money.

"They're making a break for it! Circle around to the back!"

"Wait, there's still one straggler! She's trying to grab the club's money! Deal with her first!"

As Alice and I bolt out the back door, shouting can be heard coming from inside.

"There, we've captured the greedy one! We'll interrogate this one and get the details!"

"Y-you lot, do you know who you're dealing with?! State your unit, titles, and names! I'm the former knight captain of the Royal Guard, and...!"

"Stop resisting! Don't try to hide the money in your dress! Let go!"

With Snow staying back and buying us time, we make our way from that spot—

3

The next day...

After making a safe exit, we've quickly given up on the hostess club scam and switched to a new hustle.

"We made the mistake of using someone as greedy as Snow yesterday. But we won't let it end here. Leave it to me. I've got an idea."

"Boss, I'm sorry, but I can't imagine this going well. Can I go home?"

I figured Snow would be back pretty quickly after that since it was a pretty minor offense, but she's evidently refusing to hand back the money and is still in custody.

Sure, we were the ones who told her it'd be a profitable gig, but she was the most enthusiastic about the work, which might mean she's further gone than I first thought.

Still, it's only the second day of the festival.

I'm sick of the fact that my point total is negative and want to do something about it while the festival's still going on.

"Aw, don't say that, Rose. We're comrades, aren't we?"

"That's right. We're already coconspirators, and we sink or swim together. It's too late for you to back out."

"Wait, Miss Alice, what do you mean coconspirators? I'm going home! W-wait, why are you two grabbing me? Please stop! Let me go!"

Alice and I put our hands on Rose's shoulders as she tries to leave.

"Now wait, Rose; we're counting on you. The term *coconspirator* Alice used doesn't mean much. If anything, we can't call this an evil deed at all."

"If you help us out, I'll make sure you get all the food you can eat. The job's simple. Get inside this animal suit and fawn on the person we specify."

We then point to a dog suit, a small one designed to fit someone of Rose's size.

"I—I won't be fooled! I keep telling you that you can't just buy me off with food!"

I gently pat Rose as she looks at us with suspicion. "Rose, you were raised by your grandpa, right? The person we want you to fawn on is an old man who lost a family member."

Rose freezes.

Alice follows up with her own details.

"The geezer's been waiting every year for his family to visit him. Sadly, they haven't shown up once. So we just want you to pretend to be his family member who's come back for the Undead Festival. Y'know, make him feel good."

"…All right, I understand. I'll help, if that's the case. You two really are unfair! There's no way I could say no to that…"

Rose lets out a troubled laugh and climbs into the animal suit.

"I knew you'd say that, Rose. You're a good egg."

As I say that and smile, the stuffed animal glances away a little shyly—

"I've brought him like you asked. Your dear little Patrasche... Hey, Patrasche, calm down. Sit! Patrasche, sit!"

"...! ...!! ...!!!"

I try to hand the suited Rose to the old man, but Rose puts up some fierce resistance.

As Rose grabs the rope around the stuffed animal's neck and tries to tear it off, I say in a hushed tone, *"Knock it off, Patrasche! I thought you were here to console the old man!"*

"You said I'd be posing as his family, so I assumed you meant a grandchild or something! But this...Patrasche?! It's a pet! It's most definitely a pet! No wonder it didn't come back!"

Yes, turns out the old man lost his pet dog.

I don't know where she found the assignment, but Alice snagged the request to find the dog.

I guess this old man's one of the richest people in the city, and Alice's plan is to fool the geezer and get the reward money, but...

"Patrasche...? Is that you, Patrasche?! Come here, Patrasche; let's take a walk."

"I'm glad Patrasche came back, old man. Mind paying up now?"

As the old man happily celebrates seeing Rose, Alice goes up to him to ask for the money.

Sure, this feels a bit like an *I'm your long-lost so-and-so* identity scam, but it's actually a pretty good win-win scenario where everyone but Rose, stuck pretending to be the pet, leaves happy.

"Boss, I won't forgive you for this! I'll endure it because I don't want to disappoint the poor old man, but I'll remember this when I get back!"

"All right, all right. I'll treat you to something really tasty when you get back, okay?"

"Please stop treating me like I'm some sort of hungry, hungry character!"

Whispering back at me, Rose then gets down on all fours and approaches the old man.

It's still pretty clear from her posture she's not happy with this, but she seems to have made her peace with it to please the old man.

"Patrasche, is something wrong? Why are you on all fours? Are you in pain?"

"Hey, geezer, isn't Patrasche a dog?" Alice asks.

"Patrasche is a Mounting Gorilla," the old man replies. "Very aggressive. He'd tackle anyone who looked strong, pin them in a mounting position, and beat them up—"

"Whoooooa! Patraaasche?!" I dodge out of the way as Rose suddenly lunges at me. She circles around and makes another lunge, and I fight to keep her at bay.

"Ahhh, it's Patrasche! That tackle is unmistakable! It's Patrasche!"

"Good. Great. Fantastic. Fork over the cash already."

As I grapple with the animal suit, I whisper under my breath, *"What the hell are you doing, Patrasche?!"*

"I have to be convincing! Sorry, Boss! Please let me beat you up!"

"You're taking advantage of this to attack me, aren't you?"

As I barely manage to hold her off, the old man calls over happily, "Now, Patrasche, stop playing and come with me. I've prepared all your favorite treats."

"I'm sure I don't have to tell you this, but don't you dare leave. Right now, you're Patrasche possessing the stuffed animal. Whatever he offers you, don't give into temptation—got it?"

"I'm not that much of a glutton. It'll be fine. I can bear it."

Bear it? That phrasing's already problematic.

"Patrasche, I've prepared tons of the gourmet supopocchi prime rib that you love. Even if it's just during the festival, eat as much as you can."

"Hey, Patrasche, stop! I'll give you a banana later, so stay!"

Patrasche doesn't last two seconds against the temptation of gourmet prime rib.

Do the gorillas on this planet eat meat? Wait, can I even be sure Alice's translator is working properly?

"Ha-ha, good boy, Patrasche. Miss Alice, here's the reward. Please accept it."

"Thanks." Alice happily accepts the money.

Meanwhile, easily tempted by the food, Patrasche happily leaves with the old man.

4

Today's the third day of the Undead Festival.

Snow is evidently still in custody, refusing to return the money and demanding to see a lawyer.

Alice, who has completely memorized this kingdom's laws, has volunteered for the position. She was enthusiastically stating how she was going to exploit all the loopholes, so it looks like that gold digger will be released soon.

As for Patrasche, now that she's been adopted by the old man, she probably won't be back for the duration of the festival.

Which means I'm stuck here alone without anything to do.

"You're an odd one. Coming back to order skewers from us after seeing that exchange. Even I have to admit I'm surprised."

"Hey, I promise not to get angry, so tell me what this meat is, will you? My curiosity's killing me."

I've been sniffing the mystery meat skewers from the guy Snow had demanded a bribe from.

I don't smell anything particularly wrong with the meat, but I'm not convinced it's safe to eat.

I mean, this rock's inhabitants eat all sorts of weird things, including mokemokes and pyokopyokos. Maybe the attitude toward this meat is just a cultural difference.

"Just to confirm, this isn't something like human meat, right?"

"Now, why would you say such a thing?! Of course not!"

Based on how offensive the suggestion is to the owner, it looks like the coast is clear on that front.

In which case, given all the things I ate as part of my survival back on Earth, there's nothing that'd cause much of a problem for me.

I open my mouth to take a bite.

"Of course it's not something as normal as human meat..."

"Wait, what did you just say?"

As I lower the skewer from my mouth...

"Found you, Commander! Tch, where the heck have you been? Leaving me to fend for myself!" Grimm squeakily rolls up in her wheelchair with a big frown on her face. I'm surprised to see her awake and moving around this early in the morning. She glances at the skewer I'm holding. "I bought you food under the implied promise that you'd help me out! The others who might help out, like Snow and Rose, are nowhere to be found, either!"

Grimm grumbles and grabs the skewer out of my hand.

"Oh!"

And then...

"Besides, like I told you last time, managing the Undead Festival is work assigned by the kingdom! It's your whole unit's responsibility, not just mine!"

""""Uh…""""

Grimm takes a bite as the owner and I look on.

I have no idea what creature the mystery meat came from, but at the very least, it doesn't appear to be poisonous.

"…Uh, here, I'll give you the rest of these skewers. So cheer up, okay?"

"Oh, thank you. What is it, Commander? Are you finally coming around to my charms?"

Grimm's mood turns quickly at something as simple as someone buying her meat skewers. I guess she's so starved for kindness from men that even a minor meal is a cause for celebration.

Eventually, the woman with strategic-level baggage seems to get a weird notion into her head, squirming from side to side in a way that sets off alarm bells in my mind.

"Say, Commander. Why don't we go on another date? All you have to do is help me out a little first!" She then breaks out into a bright smile.

"Save it."

It seems she can't understand my reply, and she continues, oblivious…

"So for this next date, we can start with a walk by the river…"

"Wait, why?! You've got a catch like me asking you out! Given the circumstances, you should accept!"

"You're not a catch; you're a virgin slut and quite possibly the thirstiest person I've ever met… Hey! What are you doing? Let go of my belt!"

Forced to tag along with Grimm, I'm now pushing her wheelchair along the road by the river.

"Say, Commander, walking together like this, don't you think we look like a couple?"

"We look like a sickly patient and her caretaker," I fire back.

Grimm furrows her brow in a frown. "You know, I noticed this a while ago, Commander, but you're a Snow-level *tsundere*, aren't you?

She can't really help it, since she's had to compete against men all her life, but what happened to you to make you so stubborn?"

"I'm not stubborn. I'll follow a good-looking woman like a lemming, and if the price is right, I'll go out of my way to do things for them. Any woman I reject just isn't worth the effort, or she's not attractive to begin with."

Grimm sets her arm on the wheelchair's armrest and tilts her head with a little smile.

"You're definitely stubborn, Commander. Let me rephrase it, then. Say, Commander, could you please give me a hand with my work? And once we're done... Let's go out for a night on the town again."

"Any woman I reject just isn't worth the effort, or she's not attractive to begin with."

"You've got a beauty like me offering you a date in exchange for your help; what's the deal?! All right, fine—I'll take you to the bar we went to the other night and buy us a bottle of the best champagne!"

And now I find myself agreeing to help Grimm after she started clinging and pleading with me tearfully, but...

"Honestly, I think your mistake is asking for my help. I'll be blunt. I know nothing about this country's laws or customs."

"Yeah, I'm not expecting your brains to be of any use, either. I'm actually hoping to borrow your brawn, Commander."

The bit about not expecting my brains to be of any use bothers me a little bit, but...

"Well, in that case, leave it to me. You want to pick fights, right?"

"No, I'm not asking you to do something that shady. It's the other way around. I want you to help keep peace in the city. Among the responsibilities for the Undead Festival's management is to stop pranks and capture misbehaving spirits."

I'm good at keeping the peace.

It might seem surprising at first, but Combat Agents are used to keep order in conquered territories.

Keeping order makes establishing authority that much easier.

So long as it's peaceful and the economy is thriving, people really don't care who is in charge.

"Not to mention… I've been saying this for a while, but there's something odd about this year's Undead Festival. There's usually not this much trouble…" Grimm mentions something of interest.

"Trouble?"

For us, trouble is part of our business, but unfortunately, we're not in Japan at the moment.

Grimm shoots me a look full of concern.

"I've gotten a nonstop stream of bizarre reports. Well, for example… A stuffed animal bursting into flames in public or creepy black shadows heading toward the castle late at night. Smaller examples include scammers operating out of the business district…"

This all sounds familiar.

"The rest sound like urban legends, to be honest… Like the prime rib that mysteriously disappeared after being offered to a certain doll, and something about a scary skewer stall selling mystery meat…"

Yup, that sounds familiar, too.

"More than anything else, I'm getting reports that dolls are attacking people. With me in charge, that shouldn't be happening, given that spirits have to sign a contract before they get to possess one."

I recall that I recently got tackled by a doll named Patrasche.

"Grimm, I think you can just ignore those problems."

"Why?! Have you been listening to me?! They might all sound

like jokes to you, but there are victims here! It's not like I'm making things up!"

Grimm's not lying; I know that better than anyone.

"I see; this year's Undead Festival sounds like a doozy. You know, just yesterday, Alice and I did a small side gig, so I've got a little spending money. Why don't I treat you today, as your commander, in recognition of all your hard work?"

"Why are you saying that all of a sudden?! I worry I'll fall in love when a man's nice to me, so please don't do that."

I keep pushing Grimm in her wheelchair as she starts to panic.

"So what do you want to do after a walk by the river? Do you have somewhere you'd like to go?"

"Now you even sound nicer! U-um, well, after a walk by the river, maybe a picnic in the park…"

The park's currently our temporary hideout.

"I didn't pack a lunch today, so no picnics. I've got a decent bit of money, so how about I buy you a necklace? Let's head to a jewelry store."

"I'd love to…"

I push the wheelchair onward as Grimm falls silent for some reason.

5

Floating on cloud nine, Grimm starts speaking to me.

"Say, Commander? I've been thinking this awhile, but you're pretty caring. And you don't discriminate against people like me or Rose who aren't quite human. That's actually really attractive."

"Oh yeah? Feel free to praise me some more."

If my response bothers her at all, the current Grimm gives no sign of it.

"I actually think that confidence of yours is also pretty attractive,

Commander. You're strong and dependable, but you're also mysterious and have your share of secrets... Your perverted streak is a little annoying, but...you're a man, after all. You can't help it. Besides, the fact that you sexually harass me a lot means you think I'm attractive, right?"

"Whoa, look at that rack on that chick— Huh? Yeah, sure. What were we talking about again?"

Grimm chuckles softly at my distraction as I push the wheelchair.

"Are you suddenly shy, Commander? Pretending not to hear. That part of you is also cute and attractive, you know?"

"I think that's the first time I've been called cute since I was running around as the Fly."

I don't want to think about what they were calling *cute* in that instance.

"I never dreamed it'd turn out like this with you, Commander... Especially since you hiked up my skirt when I first met you. I was beside myself with anger, wondering what sort of person would do that to someone they just met..."

"That was because you were trying to show me your panties. That's not my fault."

"Heh-heh, I had no intention of actually showing you. Oh, just so we're clear, I'm not some floozy who shows everyone my underwear! You're actually the only one who's seen it, Commander!" Grimm hurriedly adds, as though making excuses.

What's gotten into her?

I mean, it's none of my business who Grimm shows her underwear to...

"Commander, let's go into this shop!"

The shop Grimm points us to must cater to younger couples, as none of the items are particularly pricey.

Now if I were here with Snow, I bet she'd go to some expensive shop and ask for all sorts of overpriced trinkets...

"We can go somewhere higher end. I'm kind of loaded right now, actually."

Given that most of the complaints she's getting aren't actually her fault, I'd prefer to properly make it up to her.

But for some reason, Grimm just blushes.

"P-please don't spoil me like that. I don't want you to think I'm some sort of gold digger... And I know I'm clingy. If you're that nice to me, I don't think I'll be able to turn back."

"I think you're already well past the point of no return."

There's certainly a lot of oddballs in Kisaragi, but we don't have that many women with her kind of baggage.

At my comment, Grimm's blush deepens, and she tucks her knees into her chest, huddling into a bundle in her wheelchair.

"Ahem, if you two could please stop flirting in front of the store—you're getting in the way of our business. Please step inside," an employee who had been watching our exchange suddenly calls out to us.

Grimm's face goes beet red, and she casts small glances up at me from time to time.

"Mm, how obnoxious! So how can I help you today?" The employee's smile doesn't so much as twitch. If that's their approach to customer service, why even work at a place like this?

Grimm looks down, saying in a faint whisper, "U-um... We're here to buy a necklace."

"My, my, my, a necklace! May Lord Zenarith curse you! Oh, my apologies. How lovely! Congratulations!"

Uh, pretty sure I heard the dark god's name just now, but Grimm doesn't seem to notice.

Actually, there was something else I was wondering about.

"Hey, Grimm, why's this person getting so worked up over a necklace?"

""......""

The pair go silent, and I even feel the scrutiny of the other customers who had been browsing in the store.

"...Sir, are you and this young lady not in a relationship?"

"Huh? She's just my subordinate. I've caused her some problems, so I figured I'd buy her some jewelry as an apology. But I figured she'd get the wrong idea if I gave her a ring, so that's why I settled for a necklace."

At these words, Grimm stops breathing.

6

People walking by are starting to stare at Grimm, who's sitting in her wheelchair, knees cradled to her chest and pouting.

"Hey, Grimm, just because you're undead doesn't mean it's not surprising when you almost die on me, so can you try to be a little more careful?"

"And whose fault do you think that is?! I was so happy... It was the first time someone had liked me since my childhood sweetheart sent me a love letter when I was little...! Heck, I still keep that love letter as a precious memento. That's how important it was to me!"

I'm pretty sure Rose used that love letter as an offering when bringing Grimm back to life...

Grimm hasn't quite settled down from her excitement. She keeps touching the object around her neck, even as she grumbles. The necklace is cheap, and she glares balefully each time she spots a couple walking down the street.

"Cheer up already. I told you I didn't know anything about this kingdom's laws or customs. And you said you didn't expect anything from me in that area. How was I supposed to know that necklaces are an engagement token? I'd never heard of that."

"I didn't know you were such a numbskull, Commander! Necklaces imply things like *I'm attached to you* or *I'm putting a collar around you to claim you as my own*. You're such a womanizer! A womanizer unaware of how much damage he does!"

Oh, c'mon...

"I'm not trying to seduce you, you know; you're just too clingy."

"How can you say that? After treating me so sweetly! And as a reward for causing me a little trouble? Sure, you made me buy you all those drinks at the bars and wandered home after hitting on another woman. Still, that's not enough to merit a necklace. Oh, you're most certainly a womanizer! If you can't take responsibility, don't be so sweet to me!"

That wasn't what I meant in terms of trouble, but...

"Oh, whatever; I'm sorry. Now give me back that necklace, I'll go trade it for another piece of jewelry."

"Commander, what are you talking about?! Not only are you going to disappoint me, you're going to rob me of my necklace as well?! I was planning to celebrate the first necklace I ever received as a gift, but I guess I'm not allowed such a fleeting moment of joy, am I?"

Oh, for the love of— This chick is a pain in the ass!

"If we're both single a decade from now, I'll take you, all right? Now look at me, please."

Grimm, who had been looking away and pouting in her wheel-chair, suddenly turns her head toward me.

"What do you mean 'take me'? Just who do you think you are?! And a decade?! You're saying that I still won't be married by then?! You better sign a real contract saying you'll marry me in ten years if we're both single!"

"You really are a handful. This is what I mean by 'clingy.'"

Producing a sheet of paper out of who knows where, Grimm begins writing.

Is she seriously drawing up a contract?

Wondering where she got the piece of paper, I look closely at the wheelchair and notice a little accessory bag on its side.

Peering inside, I see signed forms for marriage applications.

"…Just so we're clear, I do have someone I like. So don't get your hopes up too much."

"You have someone already, and yet you were hitting on me? Just what is wrong with you, Commander? Still, I don't mind. Whoever she is, I'm sure she'll dump you."

Does she want to get smacked?

"Stamp your blood print here… Hmm, ten years is a really long time, isn't it? Surely there's a way we can speed things along?"

"Nope, not at all. And you do recognize that the way you stamp your blood print without hesitation is part of why no one wants you, right?"

Seriously, she'd be a catch if it weren't for the cursing, the clinginess, and the overall sense of desperation.

"I'm not someone who just wants to marry the first man who comes up, you know. I'm only saying this because I don't dislike you, Commander. Like I said earlier, you treat Rose like a normal person. That really is attractive. Now write your name here and stamp your blood print here."

"You know, you're almost charming when the subject's Rose. Why can't you just keep that going?"

I ignore Grimm's constant nagging to press my blood print and instead just put my signature onto the contract.

"All right, you feel better now? Why don't we start on keeping the peace around town?"

"I can't quite accept that you won't sign in blood, but oh well. I'll curse you if you break your promise. All right, let's go tackle the problems one by one."

*   *   *

First, Grimm leads us to the park we've been staying at.

Grimm glances around, seeming to have noticed something. Then she nods.

"Here's our first stop. Apparently, a doll burst into flame. Usually, that would be impossible. But since we're in the middle of the Undead Festival, I actually have a theory. Someone who had powerful magical abilities in life became a spirit and…"

"Oh, that was Heine dressed up in an animal suit. She put on a costume and snuck in. When we tried to pin her, she set her costume on fire with her powers."

……

"Why didn't you say that earlier?! I look like an idiot for taking it seriously."

"You can't put that on me. You were the one who was so sure of herself. If anything, you should be praising me for stopping Heine after she snuck into the city!"

Grimm starts bumping into my legs but eventually regains her composure.

"O-of course, you're right; you were defending the city, Commander… Oh well, to the next spot!"

With that, we make our way toward the next scene.

Our next stop was…

"Here. For some reason, the prime rib left in front of a stuffed animal in this estate keeps disappearing."

As I feared, it's the old man's house where Rose is.

Grimm approaches the gatekeeper and calls out.

"I'm Grimm, the administrator for the Undead Festival. I'm here to investigate reports of unexplained supernatural phenomena."

"Oh, you're here at last! Please come inside. The master keeps saying it's just Patrasche eating the food, but of course, there's no way a stuffed animal can eat…"

As we're led inside, there on the sofa, a stuffed animal is lying around like a cat, happily indulging in head pats from the old man.

Seeing this, Grimm's expression twitches. "…Rose?"

"?!"

The doll flinches, sensing that the jig is up.

Noticing the sharp reaction, the old man petting Rose looks over at us. "Ah, guests? Oh, you were here the other day…!"

"Wait, you've met before?! Commander, what's going on?"

"It's exactly what it looks like."

My immediate reply tells Grimm everything she needs to know, and she frowns.

"That's Rose, isn't it? We've known each other too long for you to trick me! …Stop—you can't fool me by walking on all fours and pretending to be a pet."

She glares at Rose who begins to put on an elaborate act next to the old man.

"Just what do you think you're doing? This is disrespectful to the dead! Stop messing around. We're going home."

As Grimm tries to make her way to Rose, the old man steps in front of her.

"What are *you* doing? Who said you could barge into my home and yell at Patrasche?"

"What do you mean, Patrasche? That's Rose."

"Don't be ridiculous! How do you explain this strength if this isn't Patrasche? All my servants who held on to doubt were thoroughly convinced after he tackled them. Whatever you might say, this is Patrasche. This is our Patrasche!"

Rose stands up, and I remember she was raised by her grandpa and has been thoroughly spoiled as of late.

She turns to Grimm—

"Eeep! Wh-what are you doing, Rose?! You know what'll happen if you do this— Ow! Ow, ow! Okay, okay, Patrasche! You're not Rose; you're Patrasche! I won't say anything else, so please let me go!"

After Patrasche tackles her and puts her into a choke hold, Grimm quickly taps out. It seems Patrasche will be staying here for the rest of the festival.

She really enjoys doing nothing but eating, lazing around, and getting spoiled by an old man.

As soon as she's released, Grimm hides behind my back.

"You better watch out, Rose! Once the Undead Festival's over, I'll curse you so that you can't eat anything for a whole day... I'm kidding, I'm kidding! Commander, let's go to our next stop." Grimm suddenly starts speaking faster, as though trying to avoid the doll that's suddenly started rushing toward her.

After leaving the old man's manor, we find ourselves at Tillis's place.

"Late at night, there's been creepy shadows making their way toward the castle..."

"Oh, those were our Combat Agents. Until a few days ago, sneaking into Tillis's room without waking her was the big thing for our guys."

Grimm casts a questioning gaze in my direction. "...Commander? So far, all the incidents have involved people we know. You wouldn't happen to know anything about the other reports, would you?"

"The only other thing I can think of is that Snow was caught for being the ringleader of that rip-off hostess club... Hey, don't sleep here; at least get in your wheelchair."

Grimm collapses in a heap, falling from the wheelchair to the ground.

"Seriously...? I put in all this effort, running around trying to solve these problems, and they're all caused by people I know…! About the only thing left is the shady stall selling mystery meat…"

I'm tempted to tell her that she's already eaten a skewer from that shop, but I'm pretty sure she'd yell at me for not saying something sooner.

"Which is why I bought you that necklace. Given how happy you were at first, we're even, right?"

"Of course not! If I'd known you'd done all this, I would've asked for something fancier!"

Just as Grimm starts yelling at me, the nearby dolls move to surround us.

"See?! They all agree with me! They're here to protest your poor treatment!"

"This is the cutest protest I've ever seen. I won't surrender to this. If anything…"

Just as I start to comment on the dolls around us, Grimm's empty wheelchair gets swatted aside and makes a loud crash.

I look over to see what's going on—

"Hey, Commander, who's inside that one? I promise not to get mad if you'll tell me."

"I…I really don't know this time! I don't know anyone that fancy!"

Standing there is a cat-shaped stuffed animal holding a metal club.

"Being an Underboss Is a Rough Job"

Thank you all for your letters.

I was happy to learn just how much you three love me.

There's a lot to deal with on this planet.

As for details, there's a lot more women than men because of the war.

Which means I'm popular. Really, really popular.

The spinster named Grimm is head over heels for me. We recently got engaged.

The young Lolita named Rose almost devoured me when we were stranded in the desert.

A well-endowed woman named Snow keeps using every opportunity she can to show off her boobs.

She's already kissed me.

I'll also include a progress report: Because the Undead Festival is underway, we opened a boob-centric hostess bar. Stuffed animals started bursting into flames, and Patrasche tackled me, but I managed to gain the upper hand, somehow.

Recently, the fad among the Combat Agents is to hold barbecues next to sleeping beauties.

Since so much has happened, I had to give you the abridged version, but that's the gist of what's going on. Did you follow all that?

Agent Six

1

Weaving between the wandering dolls, I run like hell through the streets of Grace.

"Hey, Commander, could you hold on a moment?! Wait, wait, please; my underwear's going to show!"

"Why are you worrying about that now? It's hardly the time! Besides, I've seen your underwear countless times! It's a little late to be embarrassed!"

After getting ambushed by that mysterious stuffed animal, I'm trying to make my way back to the temporary hideout in the park. With her wheelchair destroyed, I'm hauling Grimm over my back.

"Dammit, what the hell was that thing? It's heavy, rock-solid, and OP as hell! There's no way we can beat it without a decent weapon!"

It's just another stuffed animal.

With that thought in mind, the first thing I tried was kicking it.

But that cat doll blocked the blow with the metal club, coordinating with other dolls to counterattack.

Then I thought to grapple with it and tear it to shreds. But for some reason, it had a lot of mass for a stuffed animal, and its monstrous strength was even greater than mine with my power armor. It almost broke my back.

Unfortunately, Alice has my main weapon, the R-Buzzsaw, under lock and key (although I can always get it back when I leave the city) after I attacked Tiger Man.

It might also be because when I got drunk, I chopped down a few trees they consider holy in this country, or the fact that I got drunk and tried to carve a large boulder popular with tourists into the shape of a pretty woman.

"Commander, can you at least carry me bridal style instead of giving me a piggyback ride?! My skirt keeps riding up, and at this rate, I really will be exposed! If you run around town while I'm like that, I'm really going to make you take responsibility!"

"Are you *trying* to make me ditch you?! You can run on your own feet!"

"It'd be one thing if we were inside the castle or in a building, but you'd really make a barefoot girl run around outside?! The gravel really hurts!"

Actually, wait a minute...!

"Why am I getting attacked by your dolls in the first place?! You're the leader of these undead. Do something!"

"Wh-what am I supposed to do? Sure, I made those dolls, but I don't recognize any of the spirits possessing them. I bet there's just something inside of them! Are you sure you don't have anyone who wants you dead?"

It's possible there are people inside.

I mean, there's plenty of precedent with Heine and Rose, and more than that...

"I've got way too many people who hate me. It's pointless to try and narrow them down..."

"Say, Commander, just go ahead and set me down! I can't imagine I'm not just getting caught up in your problems!"

If I leave Grimm behind, getting rid of the extra weight *would* make it easier to run.

But there's the possibility that the cat doll is holding back because I'm carrying Grimm.

For some reason, the cat doll hasn't gone all out yet.

If anything, it feels like it's watching for something…

"Come on—we're comrades, aren't we? I won't just leave you behind; trust me."

"I'm not your comrade; I'm your subordinate! I can't trust you when you're so eager to point out your rank the rest of the time! But anyway, carry me bridal style! If you're going to keep carrying me, then at least do it right! If you don't, all the men in the city will see my panties!"

With Grimm yelling into my ear, I give in and shift to carrying her the way she wants.

I punt a pig doll when it pounces on us from the side, then survey my surroundings for anything I can use as a weapon.

"…Say, Commander, what should we do? I know I suggested it, but being carried like this, even under these circumstances, makes my heart flutter…"

I toss Grimm at the cat doll that's been following us.

<Evil Points Acquired>

2

Activating the power armor's general-purpose camo feature, I use my arms to hide my face and duck into the shadow of a garbage can.

While it's not on the level of high-priced equipment like the optical camo, it's enough to let you avoid casual scrutiny.

I figured it would be fine, since she told me to leave her there, but I didn't think it'd end up this way.

"Commander, come out here! I know you're here! You have until I count to ten! If not, I'll curse you so that you won't be able to meet any attractive members of the opposite sex for at least a year!"

Yikes. Talk about suicide terrorism.

In spite of the possibility of getting hit by the curse herself, she's willing to suffer the consequences if it means she can get her revenge.

But this doesn't even rise to the level of a threat.

If I won't meet new attractive women, it just means I will focus on the ones I already know.

I'm already surrounded by women—female bosses, subordinates, coworkers, and even enemies.

I wouldn't be able to handle any more potential heroines, so I don't care if I don't meet new—

"I'm right here! Here I am! Let's just calm down!"

I raise my hands and rise from behind the garbage can.

It's better to have as many new encounters as possible.

Duh.

"You ass! I've always dreamed of being carried that way, and then you tossed me into a dumpster!"

The stuffed cat that was chasing us dodged when I threw Grimm at it, complicating the situation.

Even I wasn't planning to go that far, but…

"I get what you're trying to say, Commander. You're saying the world's spinsters should be disposed of. Heh-heh-heh… What to do? What to do? What should I do to this insufferable ass?"

"Wait, calm down. Let's negotiate. I'll introduce you to one of my lively co–Combat Agents. He's young, strong, and loyal, and he's got a promising future, too!"

Note I haven't claimed he's handsome.

Is the situation too much for even a desperate spinster to bite?

…But Grimm goes quiet for a few minutes.

"…That's the same thing the matchmaking service told me; I won't be fooled. But I suppose I can at least listen to your pitch. Depending on what you say, I might forgive you for throwing me in the trash."

Grimm is standing barefoot in the middle of the road, rooted to the spot by inner conflict, when a shadow falls across her.

The cat doll that had been following me suddenly appears behind Grimm and…

I can't shake a sense of déjà vu at the sight.

I act before I think.

I draw my pistol and shoot the cat doll in the head.

"Eeep! W-wait, Commander—what are you…?"

Behind the frightened Grimm, the cat doll keeps its club raised, reaching up and pressing its free hand to its head.

Grimm glances over her shoulder and sees what's going on, then runs toward me.

"Help, Commander! I just had a terrible flashback!"

"I feel close to remembering something, too! This is bad. That weapon looks familiar as well!"

Yes, I remember that heavy club.

I may easily forget faces and things people say, but when it comes to combat, my memory's pretty good.

Yes… There's no mistaking him.

"I remember now! That's the Battering Hero, the Golden Bat! He was a Hero who had to give up his dream of becoming a professional ballplayer after tearing a tendon, and because his name is similar to a very famous Hero, he's referred to as the Imitation Bat…"

"No, that's not it, Commander! That can't be it! Because I'm feeling déjà vu over the thing inside the cat doll, too!"

Grimm ducks behind my back, pointing her finger at the cat doll.

"You, identify yourself! If you're undead, then you can't escape Lord Zenarith's rule! And that doll's one of my masterpieces! I'm really fond of it so don't damage it... Oh no!"

Ignoring Grimm's warning, the cat doll begins to stuff the cotton spilling from the bullet hole back inside.

"What are you doing to the fruits of my labor, Commander? Do you know how much time it took to make this many dolls...?"

"This is hardly the time! The other dolls are coming closer, too! Are you sure you're a bishop or whatever?"

The dolls nearby approach and surround the cat doll, as though to shield it.

Minus the cat doll in the middle, the dolls move awkwardly, as though they're puppets on strings.

"In the name of Archbishop Grimm, I beseech you, Lord Zenarith! Remove your blessing from the undead here and return them to—"

"Stop that, dammit! How many times do you plan to kill yourself? We're out of offerings to sacrifice to bring you back to life!"

I've lost count of the number of times Grimm's done her suicide spell; pretty sure we're playing with fire here.

But Grimm tilts her head with a curious expression. "What are you going on about, Commander? Undead can't commit suicide. I'm just going to remove the blessing of undeath from them."

"Do you not remember how you've been dying lately? You keep collapsing along with the other undead!"

Seems this useless bishop doesn't remember that she was removing her own blessing each time along with the rest.

Grimm looks unconvinced. "I find it hard to believe that I, Miss Grimm, would do something so stupid... Still, there's something wrong with these dolls. They didn't even twitch at the mention of Lord Zenarith's name. There might be a necromancer inside that cat doll..."

Necromancer.

A term that describes magic users who control the dead and that conjures images of antisocial and depressive people.

But the cat doll in front of us is most definitely the warrior type.

"Nah, just from fighting with that thing, I'm pretty sure it's some sort of meathead. Necromancers are pretty smart, right? I mean this one's dumb enough to possess a cat doll."

"Not so loud—it can hear you... Hey, Commander, it seems to be quivering..."

The cat doll begins to tremble as though holding back its anger. It points its free hand toward the ground...

<Elite Four member of the Demon Lord's Army, Gadalkand of the Earth, commands you!>

I hear the order inside my head like my internal announcer.

Probably because it has no vocal cords.

<Kill all the living in this city!!>

The cat doll issues the command telepathically.

3

Running desperately through the city of Grace, I call into my headset, "This is Agent Six! I'm being chased by a weirdo! Requesting backup! Bring me a weapon! Right now, I'm in front of the bookstore where the busty girl works! Bring me a powerful weapon! OVER!"

"Owwww! My feet hurt! Commander, carry me! I don't care if it's a piggyback ride! Please carry me!" Grimm screams to me as I call for reinforcements.

"This is a good opportunity for you to toughen your feet up! What are we gonna do?! The undead are flooding the city!"

"Don't look at me! Commander, what do we do? People are going to blame *me* for this!"

Grimm's on the verge of tears, either from running around barefoot or because of the situation.

Thanks to Gaddy Lad or whatever his name is, a ton of zombies have popped out of the ground.

That's not a metaphor. They're literally popping out of the ground.

As might be expected, the citizens of the city are panicking at the sudden horde of zombies.

Some try to put up a fight; others try to run.

An old woman calls out to a zombie, asking if it's the old man from next door. It looks like she's trying to take it home with her.

"Leave that part to me. If we report the situation to Alice, who's in command, I'm sure she'll figure something out. All we need to do is keep him occupied as we wait for reinforcements. Looks like it's just the zombies attacking the people around us. Zombies may look horrible, but they don't seem overly strong, so we probably don't have to worry about the citizens getting slaughtered! ...I hope!"

"You could at least show some confidence there! You get paid to defend this country, don't you?! ...Still, I wasn't expecting Gadalkand of the Earth, one of the Demon Lord's Elite Four, to return... I let my guard down. He was controlling golems when we first faced him. I should have known he was capable of this, too..."

Grimm clicks her tongue with a dark expression on her face, but I feel like I'm still not getting the whole picture.

"You know Gaddy Lad? What's his deal anyway? He's clearly coming after me."

"He introduced himself, remember?! He's Gadalkand of the Earth! He's the Elite Four member that you killed! Demons proficient with earth magic also have a connection to undead that spring from tainted earth. I should have expected as much from an elite. He wasn't just a simple warrior type…"

Undead are earth-element focused, hmm?

I guess that's more or less the case on Earth, too.

"Now that you mention it, it's all coming back to me. He's the guy who blew your head off. When I saw him behind you with his club, I knew I'd seen this before."

"Please don't say things like 'blew your head off'! It's still kind of a touchy subject!"

Despite running barefoot next to me, Grimm seems to be holding up pretty well.

I figured that a nocturnal priestess would be a bit more of a book-worm, but we might be able to run off pretty easily—

"…Wait. What happened to the guy that was chasing us?"

I've lost track of how much we've run, but the cat doll chasing us has disappeared.

Just then, Grimm gasps with a realization.

"Oh dear! The castle! He's headed to the castle! Inside the shrine in the castle—"

At the same time, a zombie pops up in front of us to block our path.

"Graaaah!"

"Zombies aren't scary in daytime! Come at me, dammit! …Okay, I lied; that's creepy! Grimm, do something!"

"Commander, you're surprisingly useless today! In the name of Grimm, Archbishop of Zenarith…"

Seeing zombies in the light brings out all the creepy little details.

Grimm draws in a deep breath and shouts in a voice that rings throughout the city:

"To the kingdom's citizens who are visiting home from the land of the dead! Aid me in sending back your kin who are suffering all across this city! To all undead who hear me. In Lord Zenarith's name…"

"Ah! Don't, Grimm!"

Grimm takes out something like a charm, gripping it tightly, and calls for aid from the surrounding undead.

The item she retrieved must be extremely precious...

Casting her gaze down briefly to the object gripped in her hand, she declares with a little frown—

"Regain your senses and, with your mind clear, act as you will!"

4

The moment Grimm utters her spell, the charm disappears with a burst of bright light.

All the fuss around Grimm suddenly stops, leaving only silence.

The dolls that were rampaging immediately stop attacking, and one of the zombies that was approaching us suddenly starts looking around curiously...

"Wh-whaffa? Whaf's foin fon? Whaf fa feck if all liff..."

Evidently, its vocal cords are on their last legs.

The zombie notices it is the one trying to speak and looks down at its hands.

"...Whoa, I'm a fombie..."

It seems the zombie's figured out what's going on and glances around, at a loss...

Eventually, its eyes stop on Grimm.

"Lafy Frimm, Affbiffop off Fenariff... Um..."

Sounds like he wanted to say, "Lady Grimm, Archbishop of Zenarith." The zombie looks to Grimm and breaks out in a wide smile when she nods wordlessly at him.

"In the name of Lord Zenarith, I forgive your trespass from the nether realm and hereby permit you to return to your slumber."

"F-fank you..."

Her usual incompetence seems to have fled, and Grimm smiles as if to reassure the zombie, looking every bit the holy woman.

"Now go and resume your rest..."

Grimm, unfazed by the fetid smell of the zombie, reaches over and gently takes its decrepit hands in both her own.

The zombie closes its eyes as if at peace, then silently crumbles back to the earth.

Having witnessed Grimm's actions, I—

"Emergency, emergency! This is Agent Six! Grimm's been possessed! Requesting a skilled healer, over!"

"Hold on! If you're going to nitpick about my current holy state, I've got some thoughts of my own!"

Five minutes later.

<Yo, Six, come in. What's happening?>

I get an intercom message from Alice.

"Impressive, Commander. I didn't think I'd end up using this ace up my sleeve. This is an evil...er, holy item I've been praying to for a long, long time. Let's put an end to this. Now face the apex of disaster...!"

Faced with an excited Grimm, I suddenly come to my senses.

"We don't have time for this! Hey, Grimm, get yourself together! The undead are still going on a rampage! You're the festival organizer! You have no time to be playing around!"

"......?! Y-you're right! What am I doing?! No, wait! Commander, you were the one who...! Besides, you were responding pretty enthusiastically yourself!"

After returning Grimm to her senses, I report the current conditions to Alice.

"Alice, the city's a mess! I bought Grimm a necklace after she started tearfully clinging to me, and suddenly a stuffed cat that's actually Gaddy Lad attacked us, and then a zombie went *poof,* and Grimm's gone batshit insane!"

<You're making no sense. Put Grimm on the line.>

I hand Grimm the small mic and teach her how to use the intercom feature.

However, the receiver for this intercom broadcasts incoming messages directly into the Combat Agent's head, meaning I'll have to interpret Alice's side of the conversation.

"I see you're carrying more oddities. So I just need to speak into this?"

"Right. Can you explain the current situation to Alice?"

Finally caught up thanks to Grimm's explanation, Alice starts spitting orders.

<All right, I understand now. We just need to treat it like a terrorist attack on the city. I'll get Snow to take command of idle knights and Combat Agents and work on restoring order to the city. You're sure Gadalkand's heading to the castle shrine?>

"She says she'll hit the dolls with Snow and the knights. She's also asking if you're sure that Gadalkand's heading to the shrine."

"No doubt about it. That's where we've been keeping Gadalkand's head. The only reason he can act is because it's during the Undead Festival," Grimm replies with a deathly serious expression, and Alice goes quiet on the other end of the intercom. "Since it belonged to an enemy as high profile as an Elite Four member, we were cleansing the head in the shrine to eliminate any chance of Gadalkand's return. But Gadalkand harbored so much hatred that we haven't been able to complete the cleansing. The Undead Festival is when Lord Zenarith's power is at its peak. My guess is that Gadalkand's going to recover his head from the shrine and take advantage of the festival to return as a full-fledged greater undead creature."

I've abandoned thinking for myself because of the complicated discussion and ask Alice to give me a summary.

"So what does this mean?"

<He'll be at the shrine. I'll bring you a weapon, so make sure you finish him off this time.>

Alice always gives easy-to-understand explanations.

"Oh, that's no different from what I usually do. You didn't have to make it sound so complicated; you could have just explained it simply like Alice did."

"I made things pretty easy to understand! What exactly did Alice say?"

I ignore Grimm as she kicks up a fuss, turning my gaze to the castle.

"Target: hostile undead Gadalkand. Since we've got no one else who can fight today, Grimm, make sure you watch my back."

"You're going to make me walk barefoot to the castle?! Either carry me in your arms or on your back!"

Once things calm down, I'll have to figure out an easy way to carry her.

5

The road to the castle has become a hellscape.

Seeing the knights scattered here and there, Grimm lets out a cry of despair.

"Oh my…! If he's exhibiting this much power in a temporary body…"

To beat this many knights so easily—yes, I can see how remarkable that is.

"Grimm, this is starting to feel a bit hopeless. He seems a lot stronger than when I beat him. Right now, he's a doll. I don't know how I'm supposed to land a killing blow, and any hope that he's weak because he's a doll is… Well, just look…"

Just as I'm considering retreat, one of the fallen knights raises his head.

"Th-that's not what happened…"

…?

"It was the mutant Tiger Man who disabled us… Lady Snow said the enemy commander was a cat-shaped stuffed animal and that the priority was to finish it off. She sent knights in pursuit of it… The knights who didn't know Tiger Man mistook him for the enemy and attacked him, so he retaliated…"

"Where's the one who issued that order?"

The knight points to the castle, then, as if running out of strength, collapses.

Just then…

…Alice speaks in a voice loud enough to echo through the city.

"All Combat Agents and knights in the city, report to the castle immediately. Attack the cat-shaped stuffed animal on sight. It's a cat, not a tiger. Repeat, all Combat Agents and knights report to the castle!"

It seems she used a special voice amplifier; the windows in the city shake, and everyone turns toward the voice.

"…Hey, most of the problems that happened during this Undead Festival were either your fault or the faults of people you knew, Commander…"

"All right, let's head to the castle. This is all because of Snow. She ignored Alice's orders and let her hunger for glory blind her. Got it?"

"All right. This is all Snow's fault. All the problems with this Undead Festival are Snow's fault."

It's reassuring to see Grimm thinking about her own self-preservation.

As for me—

"…It's Mariel! Bloody Mary is hunting zombies!"

"Good work, Mariel! You're the true champ!"

I can hear some people yelling in the distance, although what they're saying is strange. I dash forward while carrying Grimm on my back.

"Commander, there are zombies over there, too. I'll return them to their senses; can you head there for a moment?"

"Leave it to me! …Say, Grimm, we're kind of impressive today, aren't we? Almost like heroes saving the city!"

I had always dreamed of being a hero.

I walked the path of evil thanks to a combination of no talent for heroism and those employers, but I'm a bit excited at the opportunity to feel like I'm fulfilling my childhood dream.

Grimm looks at me with a happy little smile. "There's times where you're like a purehearted little kid. I don't dislike that about you, Commander."

"That might be nice to hear, if you weren't piggybacking on me with your butt hanging out…"

"B-butt! It's still covered, right?! My skirt's not completely hiked… Oh, oh, hang on a moment! We're almost at the castle; let me fix my skirt hem!"

Grimm and I head toward the castle, stopping to bring the zombies back to their senses and convince them to return to the earth.

I'm carrying Grimm on my back, and maybe it's because I'm wearing power armor, but I'm not getting as much out of the experience as I'd prefer.

Then there's the whole comparison between Snow and Grimm…

"Hmm… Personality aside, I think I'd rather carry Snow on my back than Grimm…"

"Hey, just what part of me are you comparing to Snow?! Let me point out that mine are average. Actually, maybe even bigger than average. And I don't hold back with a man I love. You know, it's a pretty common thing, right? You start to worry after you get intimate at the start of a relationship because you wonder if he's just after your body… that sort of thing. Well, I'd never worry about anything so trivial!"

Seems I've touched some sort of nerve, and Grimm starts babbling again.

"The fact that you start defending yourself against things I haven't even said is part of what makes you so annoying."

"?!"

Carrying a shocked Grimm on my back, I head to the next group of zombies.

Despite looking like she has something she wants to say, Grimm does her task effectively.

…Sure, she's a pervert who shows off her butt while getting carried around, but every time she returns a zombie to the earth, she's got the look of a proper bishop.

"You know, if you always had that whole priestly-aura thing going on, I'm pretty sure you'd have been married ages ago."

"Wh-what do you mean, Commander? Don't say things like that. They catch me off guard. You really ought to stop toying with my emotions."

Evidently, one of the costs of her long spinster life is that she's no longer able to handle compliments.

Grimm gently holds the zombie's hand to reassure it as she returns it to the earth, giving no sign she's bothered by the zombie ichor getting on her hand.

Even though the combination of bare feet and clothes dirty from running makes her look like a homeless woman…

"If you just keep your mouth shut, I bet you'll be married within a few years."

"I'm not going to live my life that way! I'll find a nice husband who'll accept me even if I am a follower of Zenarith. And even if I stay single, I have someone who'll take me ten years from now, so it's not a big deal."

Oh great, she's taking that promise seriously!

You know, that's the sort of thing that drives men away. I really want to lecture her about that for an hour or so.

Still...

"It's getting worse the closer we get to the castle."

"Yes... S-say, Commander, being an elite demon, Gadalkand's stronger than expected. If worse comes to worst, will you protect me? It's possible his powers as a necromancer are greater than mine."

There's battered dolls scattered all around us, all people who died protecting this kingdom.

And now, even when visiting after death, they've sacrificed themselves again in their kingdom's time of need.

They must have thrown themselves in front of Gadalkand as he headed to the castle, holding him off as they were battered.

Grimm stops to embrace each of the dolls, whispering something to them before setting them back down.

"Seriously, if only you'd show this side of you more often..."

"...? Hmm? What is it?"

Men are pretty weak toward women who have different sides to them, but if I told her that, I feel like she'd spent every waking moment cleansing the undead.

It's attractive because she shows her hidden side every once in a while, but I can just see her overplaying the whole "holy woman" thing.

"Never mind. Anyway, we're almost at the castle. Are you ready? There aren't many zombies or dolls left; we're almost to the main target."

"I know. I'll use my secret weapon if things get desperate."

Grimm then takes something from her breast pocket.

It's a necklace for a child, the very item she tried to use in our earlier battle. She must have started carrying it in her breast pocket after she started worrying people would think she was too old for it.

"Cursing people extracts a cost. Of course, the more important the object, the better. This is a gift I was given as a child by my childhood sweetheart."

…I have a bad feeling about this.

"If it's that precious, put it away. Once Alice gets here, we'll manage somehow."

In fact, please keep it as your most precious memento for years to come.

Otherwise, it'll seem like you're okay letting it go because you recently got a necklace that can take its place…

"No, it's all right. I have the new necklace you gave me, Commander. Childhood memories should stay memories. I can't be tied down by the past forever; it's time for me to move forward!"

"Hey, you do remember what I said, right? I said I'll take you if you're still single ten years from now. If you find someone good in the meantime, go get 'em, okay?"

"I wonder how you are these days. When we were five, you said you'd marry me when we grew up, yet you so easily fell to the wiles of a big-breasted woman the moment we hit puberty. Are you happy now…?"

"Hey, can you stop it with the whole *I've found someone new, so I'll live my life moving past you* sort of vibe?"

6

"I'll walk on my own feet from here. It feels like we have a fight coming up. I'd just get in your way if you had to carry me."

"It's a little late to try and convince me that you're low-maintenance… There's someone here."

As we approach the castle's main gate, I notice someone fighting.

"Mwa-ha-ha-ha-ha! None shall pass! Die by the hand of Flame Zapper the Third!"

Snow is enthusiastically burning the stuffed animals and zombies approaching the gate.

"Grimm, I've got an eye on our guy. I'll leave the zombies and dolls to you. I'll go capture the puppet master responsible."

"Of course, leave them to me. Please make sure you apprehend the culprit," Grimm responds in a low voice as she approaches the zombies.

"You two are too late! I've already claimed all the credit! Mwa-ha-ha-ha-ha, look around you! All this speaks to my contribution! But this is only the beginning. The enemy leader is a cat-shaped stuffed animal. The knights are currently looking for it. On my command! No doubt it's only a matter of time before the enemy commander falls!"

With an ecstatic Snow in front of us, Grimm and I exchange nods.

"Raaaah! Surrender, you villain!" I grab the cackling Snow.

"Wha—?! Six, how dare you!"

"Commander, hold her like that for a bit! There, there, it's all right now. There's no more need to fight against your will. Leave everything to me and return to your rest."

After making sure Snow's been restrained, Grimm returns the undead to their senses.

Carrying out her task of returning the undead to the ground, she approaches the struggling Snow.

"You bastards! Have you gone mad?! To think you'd let your greedy intentions to steal my glory lead you to such low ends! Have you no shame?!"

"I—I don't know why, but that really hurts coming from Snow..."

As Grimm lightly presses her hand to her chest, I step in to read out the charges.

"Hey, Snow. You've really done it this time."

"Eh? What are you talking about? I've done nothing... Oh! Y-you bastard...!" Snow suddenly has a look of regret on her face, evidently finally realizing what she's done. "So you intend to bring up the hostess club scam, huh? Ah, I get it now; you'll keep quiet about the scam if I split the reward for my achievements in this battle. That's the deal, is it? Very well. Now, as for our individual shares…"

"No, that has absolutely nothing to do with what I'm talking about… You seem a little too quick to bring up hush money. Do you have a lot of experience with this or something?"

Snow goes briefly silent at my words. "…If this isn't about hush money, then what's the big idea?"

"You ordered the knights to go hunting for a cat doll even when Alice told you to focus on maintaining order, didn't you? The knights mistook Tiger Man for the cat doll and got wiped out. That's caused all sorts of problems that we're dealing with now—the city's in chaos, and we've completely lost track of the cat doll."

……

"You've got it all wrong; just listen to me."

"All right, I'll let you tell your side later. In a nice, comfy dungeon cell. Okay?"

The restrained Snow starts struggling. "I had no choice! I can't lose Her Highness's trust! I was under investigation until recently! Which means the only option I had left was to restore my reputation by producing results!"

Welp, she's finally just decided to own up to it.

"You're barely average as a field commander. We don't need you trying to do more than you're told! Thanks to you, we had to take care of the dolls and zombies in the city on our own. Hey, have you been here the whole time? You sure you haven't let a doll past?"

"I guarded the gate properly, so there's no problem at all. This main gate's currently the only way into the castle, after all. I've been standing here the whole time, so it's fine."

At Snow's words, Grimm and I let out sighs of relief.

It seems we've avoided the worst-case scenario of Gadalkand getting into the castle.

Which means all we have to do is tighten our defense of the entrance and exit points and wait for our Combat Agents to hunt down the stuffed animal.

…Snow seems to have decided that struggling is useless and instead addresses me in a conciliatory voice.

"Six, why don't we cut a deal? I was only told a cat-shaped stuffed animal lost control and started going on a rampage in the city. Could this be the Demon Lord's Army's fault?"

…Huh, she's pretty sharp considering she doesn't know any of the details.

Thinking back on it, she also correctly figured out I was a spy even though she hadn't known me very long.

I keep thinking of her as just a gold digger, but I suppose there's more to her than…

"Yes, this must be the Demon Lord Army's fault. Indeed, there's nothing else it could be. Surely, Heine of the Flames, who fell victim to monsters in the wastes, has used the Undead Festival to return and get her revenge. It's perfectly plausible that one of the Demon Lord's Elite Four knows how to control the dead. In which case, this entire string of events is sabotage activity by the Demon Lord's Army… That would about cover it, no? If you'll accept, I'll give you one of the beautiful swords from my collection. Not a bad deal, is it?"

I feel like she owes me an apology for the fact I felt even the faintest glimmer of admiration.

Just then…

…a bell tolls from inside the castle.

At the same time, I also hear objects colliding somewhere near the courtyard.

"…So much for 'none shall pass,' huh?"

"What's with that look? Believe me! It's true—I swear! I've been here the whole time, and there shouldn't be any other ways inside!"

Feeling my scrutiny, Snow desperately tries to explain.

Grimm looks at Snow, tilting her head a moment. "But this is the alarm that sounds when an unholy presence like a demon or the undead gets into the castle… Wait, don't look at me like that! I'm not an unholy presence! I'm not fully undead yet!"

…Which means the one causing the commotion must be…

7

Opening the main gate and looking inside, there are two stuffed animals duking it out.

"Hey."

"N-n-no, I was keeping a proper watch!" Snow protests. "They must have gotten in from somewhere else! …But this castle's surrounded by an outer wall; I wonder how they got in…"

That jogs my memory.

I drove stakes into the outer wall to sneak into Tillis's room.

Oh yeah, I forgot to retrieve those.

"Tsk, how do you plan to fix this, Snow? You can't keep the peace in the city with the knights; you let an intruder waltz into the castle…"

"Hold on, Grimm; leave it there. Now's not the time to point out Snow's failures. We should do something about those two stuffed animals going at it." A reasonable point, if I do say so myself.

Grimm and Snow are instantly suspicious.

"Are you involved with this, too?"

"Explain this later, okay, Commander?"

"But I haven't said anything yet." I ignore the questioning gazes from the pair and take a closer look at the dolls.

The first is a cat-shaped stuffed animal holding a unique metal club. That one's probably Gadalkand.

The problem is the other doll that's facing him.

I could swear I've seen that dog-shaped doll before…

"Oh! Say, Commander, isn't that Patrasche?!"

That's right—that's Patrasche!

For some reason, Patrasche is here. Maybe its owner, the old man, ordered Patrasche to save the city?

"Six, who is this Patrasche?"

"Patrasche is Patrasche—the Mounting Gorilla Patrasche, to be precise!"

"Wh-what was she thinking…?"

The stalemate between Patrasche and Gadalkand ends when Patraches notices us and aggressively charges in. Maybe it thinks it can leave things up to us if it loses.

A tackle aimed low takes out Gadalkand's legs.

Patrasche then swiftly straddles the enemy, landing punches without any hesitation.

"Good work, Patrasche! Keep it up!"

"Try to get it into a hold! Then you can leave the rest to me!"

"Again, who the hell is Patrasche?"

As we cheer on from the sidelines, Patrasche casts a quick glance our way.

It seems like a glance for help, even…

Just then, Gadalkand lets go of his long club, instead punching at his assailant.

Gadalkand doesn't seem to have suffered any damage from all the blows, and a realization hits me.

"Oh, duh, there's no way punches would work. His body is just a stuffed animal!"

"Oh, right! Rose, we're coming!"

We had decided to kick back and take it easy since it looked like Patrasche was winning, but we now hurry over to the dog doll.

"Rose?! Why are you bringing up her name all of a sudden?!"

Snow, who is the only one who doesn't understand what's going on, follows along as well.

<*Graaaaaaaaah!*>

"?!"

Patrasche takes a heavy kick to the stomach that launches it quite some distance.

"Hey, Rose, you don't have to be Patrasche anymore! If it hurts, you can say so!"

"Th-that hurts…! He kicked me really hard; just what is that thing?"

Patrasche, aka Rose, holds her stomach while getting to her feet.

Snow sees her moment and steps in.

"I have no idea why Rose is here dressed like that, but if the enemy's a flammable stuffed animal, it's time for me to offer my assistance."

Snow's guard comes all the way down, now assuming the enemy is a mere stuffed animal.

Dropping into a fighting stance as flames burst forth from Flame Whatever, Snow cries out with all the bravado of a real hero, "I have no idea who or what you are, but you'll have plenty of time to regret crossing my path in the afterlife!"

"That's Gadalkand in there. The elite demon Gadalkand. The one Rose and Grimm fought before. He's back *from* the afterlife."

Snow freezes without a word.

<*Ga-ha-ha, ba-ha-ha-ha-ha-ha-ha! Yo, long time no see, you maggots. Glad to see so many familiar faces!*>

Picking up the club from the ground, Gadalkand starts talking to us with his annoying telepathy.

Finally figuring out the identity of her opponent, Snow breaks out in a cold sweat and starts backing away.

Meanwhile, I take a step out in front of the others as they stand on guard. "Hey, hey, hey, that's quite the makeover you've gotten,

Gadalk-whatever! I think this is a big improvement from before! I bet your old form had women running away screaming! At least now they might talk to you!"

Gadalkand twitches when he hears my taunts.

I know his type.

Cocky, arrogant, short-tempered, and violent.

It's a classic thug personality that's pretty common among Kisaragi's ranks.

<...And whose fault is it that I look like this, huh? I've been waiting. It's been a long, long wait! I spent each and every moment thinking of how I'd get my revenge on you—on all of you! If not for the Undead Festival, I might have lost my identity. But I'm lucky. I got back to the world of the living through the festival, and I've acquired this body and new powers...>

"You're pretty chatty, aren't you? You used to be a bit more of the type who wouldn't listen to what others had to say."

Gadalkand goes silent at my additional teasing. The club in his hand is quivering now; I'm guessing he's trying to rein in his anger and regain his calm.

<...Heh. Heh-heh. Ah-ha-ha-ha-ha-ha-ha, is this how you're trying to buy time? You think there's help on the way? Is that the plan?>

Whoa, he's suddenly gotten really cocky.

"Okay, you're clearly plotting something. I'll bet it's one of two clichés. Either you've got an ace up your sleeve, like reinforcements on the way, or you're not at full power yet and you have another transformation in the pocket. So which is it? I'm sure one of those is right. If not, then I can at least give you credit for originality."

Looks like I struck a nerve, and Gadalkand stops moving for a moment.

<...I'll wipe that smirk off your face soon enough.>

"Hey, look—I got it right! He's panicking! Well, damn, it's just another cliché. How disappointing. You're such a letdown!"

He's not the sort that's good at resisting taunts.

As I wind him up, Gadalkand starts losing his cool, just as I'd hoped.

"You know, Commander, I'm not sure taunting him too much is a good idea... Still, rest assured. I'm an undead specialist. If he tries to summon more undead, I'll stop him this time."

"All right, I'll leave that to you. So all I gotta do is put down this weakling."

Inspired by Grimm, Rose and Snow also take a step forward.

"Boss, leave brawling to me. I can't breathe any fire since I'm wearing a costume, but I can at least block attacks!"

"I'll keep an eye on the overall situation and stand ready to order a retreat at any moment."

It appears a certain someone has lost their nerve. Oh well.

Losing patience, Gadalkand begins moving his club from side to side.

<No matter how many weaklings you have, you're all still just weaklings. Now I see that you've got the weak Chimera brat who tried to fight me; the knight who ran away, knowing she couldn't beat me; and the undead bitch I've already killed once.>

"Hmm, yeah, guess you're right. And you were the one who got slaughtered by me, the one commanding these weaklings. They're all somewhat capable of holding their own against me. Unlike you. You went down without much of a fight at all... Huh! Guess that makes you the weakest of the bunch, huh? You're even weaker than my underlings!"

Seemingly near his limit, Gadalkand moves into a fighting stance.

"Oh, gonna come at me? There's four of us and only one of you. Not to mention you're a stuffed animal, while we have Snow's magic sword. Plus, we're just here to buy time, with the folks who heard Alice's announcement coming to reinforce us. If you're fine with all that, come on and try it. You sure you don't want to run away? Huh? Huh?"

As I continue taunting him, Snow mutters from behind me, "I really am impressed by your ability to taunt people. There are even times I feel sorry for your victims…"

It's not like I'm taunting him for the hell of it.

Sure, there's a good part of me that's doing it because it's fun, but the objective is to make Gadalkand lose his head.

What we can't afford right now is for him to abandon the doll and run.

If he returns to being a spirit and gets another body, we won't be able to tell who he is with a glance. We need to capture him somehow and conduct the exorcism while he's still trapped in the cat doll…

<*Should be about time.*>

Gadalkand starts muttering to himself.

But before I can ask *For what?* I hear the sound of a breaking window, and a scream comes from somewhere in the castle.

His objective is to retrieve his severed head.

Which means this scream is—

"Look, Six! That's not an undead; it's a demon! It's one of his lackeys!"

It's one of the demons that was flying around last time I fought Gadalkand.

Demonic statues that walk on two feet and have giant bat-like wings—commonly known as gargoyles. One of them is hovering above us, cradling something.

Seeing that, Gadalkand starts running in that direction, immediately losing interest in everything else.

As Gadalkand shows his back, Snow slashes at him without any hesitation.

"G-grrr, I won't let you do this, you walking payday! It's time for a rematch! Take this!"

As usual, I'm impressed by her skill in sneak attacks. The fact that she waits to deliver her line *after* her attack is worth a lot of praise.

<Set the head down! It doesn't matter where! As long as it's touching the ground!>

"Damn you! Look at me, Gadalkand!"

Snow drives her flaming blade into the doll's stomach, but Gadalkand pays no attention to it, reaching his hand out toward the ground.

<Gadalkand of the Earth, pillar of the Demon Lord's Elite Four, commands you maggots!>

"I, Lord Zenarith's archbishop, Grimm Grimoire command you."

Gadalkand briefly casts a baleful glance at Grimm.

<Rise, damn you!>

"Return to your slumber!"

The two shout at the same time, and nothing happens.

"Lord Gadalkand, I'll set your head down here!"

The gargoyle lackey tries to set down the object in its arms.

I draw my gun from my hip and fire at the gargoyle. The gargoyle takes the shot right between the eyes, and it, along with the head, plummets to the ground.

Just before the head hits the ground…

"Yaaa!"

…Rose lands a jump kick on it.

Engulfed in flames, Gadalkand stands there staring mutely, then slumps his shoulders.

Thanks to Rose's jump kick, the head slams into the castle wall.

Perhaps because it spent so much time in the shrine, it was more fragile than we thought and—

<Sigh, dammit. My head's been shattered.>

Gadalkand mutters offhandedly.

Without letting down my guard, I call out to our dejected foe.

"Thought you only had undead lackeys, but I see you had some living ones hidden away, too."

<Hmph, yeah, that's because the alarm rings the moment the undead enter key areas of the castle. The bell rang when I walked into the castle.>

The doll Gadalkand's possessing has become an inferno, making him look like a human-shaped fire spirit.

<Didn't you think it was odd? Where do you think I got the weapon I'm carrying?>

"Now that you mention it, that's a good point. At any rate, right now you look like a fire demon. It's kind of cool-looking," I comment, and Gadalkand turns to me.

I can't see his expression due to the flames, but it seems he's caught on to my intent.

<You buttering me up so we'll just end things here and now? I know what goes through the minds of clever little bastards like you. After all, I'm the same way.>

Seems he's not going to just let it end here.

"No, he's definitely right! You're really cool-looking right now! The very image of a fire demon! You should become the flame lord of the Demon Lord's Army!" Rose exclaims, pumping her fist. Evidently, it actually struck a chord with her. I really don't understand a Chimera's tastes.

"Well, seems we're short on time—you ready?"

<No, I'm gonna dump this body. It's true we're short on time, but elite demons can do things like this.>

The soil swells and starts forming into a person.

It looks just like the temporary vessels that Grimm used to trap those evil spirits, but those dirt dolls couldn't stay possessed for long and exploded pretty quickly. That's probably what he means when he says we're short on time.

<If there were any parts of my body left, I would have been able to swap out a dirt doll for one of those corpses and recover slowly... Oh well, even with a body like this, it's enough to drag you to hell with me.>

Even if it's made of dirt, the body is pretty much a golem.

Now that he's regained his size from when he was alive, a single blow from Gadalkand could probably break my neck.

"I don't have my main weapon today, so can I get their help as a handicap?"

<No problem. I wasn't planning to let any of you go anyway.>

Just what I'd expect from a guy in the same industry, I'll give him that much; he's a proper evil boss.

"All right, so let's do introductions... Combat Agent Six, Kisaragi Corporation."

<Gadalkand of the Earth, pillar of the Demon Lord's Elite Four! All four of you are coming with me down to the pits of hell!>

I can sense that the others behind me have dropped into fighting stances.

Since I don't have my R-Buzzsaw, I'm definitely at a disadvantage.

But this is the perfect opportunity for the power of friendship to—

"What are you guys doing?"

Suddenly, I hear the familiar voice of my partner.

If she's here, that must mean she's brought *it*.

I keep my eyes fixed on Gadalkand, but instead of reaching for the unknown entity that is the power of friendship, I reach for my trusty partner.

"Alice, this is what became of Gadalkand! He blames us for his death and came back to get his revenge! You've brought it, right?! Gimme my R-Buzzsaw!"

<Y-you! You bastard, what happened to a handicap?! And what about everything you were saying earlier...?!>

Sure, I could do the honorable thing and face Gadalkand as a true elite member of the Kisaragi Corporation, but honor ain't worth shit if you're dead.

"Oh, shut up, you moron! We're the evil Kisaragi Corporation! All that sappy crap was just an act to buy some time, obviously!"

<*Y-you bastard—you're* dead*!*>

""""Wai…!""""""

Just as everyone but Alice was about to comment on our sudden squabble…

"This world ain't big enough for two evil organizations! Time to slaughter the competition—!"

<*You son of a biiiiitch!*>

The battle was already over.

8

Despite being hacked to pieces, Gadalkand has somehow managed to keep the dirt body together and is glaring at me.

<*Don't think this is over. Ordinarily, our fight would have been the end, but with this much rage, I can sustain myself until next year's festival. You better remember this. Next time—*>

"There won't be a next time." Grimm flatly interrupts Gadalkand's last words.

<*…Stay out of this, Zenarith cultist. You're not quite human anymore, are you? What are you planning?*>

"Undeath is Lord Zenarith's specialty. There's only one thing to do here!" Grimm smiles gently at what's left of Gadalkand.

<*Are you sure you understand the risks of dealing with Zenarith? I wouldn't curse me, if I were you. Zenarith is fair. The larger the curse you try to put on someone without reason, the greater the chance it has to backfire on you. If you curse me, you're more likely to die than I am.*>

"Yes, Lord Zenarith is fair. You've killed me once, remember? No doubt the judgment will be fair."

What's left of Gadalkand goes quiet at Grimm's words.

"...Rest assured. As Archbishop of Zenarith, returning undead to the earth is part of my role. I won't use a curse."

Grimm smiles quietly, stepping toward Gadalkand.

<I'm fueled by a great sense of rage. I won't be so easily cleansed.>

As we stand on the sidelines, unable to comment, the two undead trade warning shots.

"I'll say this again: I'm the Archbishop of Zenarith. No matter how favored one may be by the Goddess of Undeath, Zenarith, I can remove the blessing from them."

<Yeah...? If you're that sure, give it a try. If it works, I'll calmly head to my rest.>

Grimm smiles gently to Gadalkand at those words.

"If you're reborn, come back as a human next time. If you're a handsome man, I'll go on a date with you."

<You're too thin for my tastes. Not enough muscle to satisfy me. I'll come back as an ogre next time as well.>

At his sarcastic words, Grimm's face has a slightly exasperated grin.

"O Great Goddess, Zenarith. I, Grimm Grimoire, your loyal servant, hereby beseech thee. Strip any blessing of undeath upon this place and return them to their eternal rest."

Clasping her hands together in prayer in the very image of a holy woman, Grimm closes her eyes, and her prayer...

...returned two undead to the soil that day.

Given the seriousness of the situation, everyone present couldn't help but stare dumbfounded at Grimm's decision to purify Gadalkand along with herself.

It's been several days since the day Grimm was summoned to Zenarith's side.

I'm at a particular spot, kneeling and offering a small prayer.

Here in this little cavern where moonlight spills in from a hole in the ceiling.

At the deepest part of the cavern is a small altar dedicated to the dark god Zenarith.

And upon that altar rests Grimm's body.

Leaving Alice to take care of the fallout from the Undead Festival, I brought Grimm's body here in the hopes of resurrecting her, offering prayers each day. However...

"I wonder if it's actually the end this time."

None of the items placed as offerings show any sign of vanishing.

Which means there's not enough sentimental items here to bring Grimm back.

Countless people offered their sentimental objects in gratitude for Grimm's efforts during the Undead Festival, but...

It seems her suicidal prayer means Grimm has been permanently sent to Zenarith's side.

Since we pledged we'd get married if we were both single a decade from now, I suppose it makes me her fiancé of sorts.

"I guess this is a case of tempting fate, too..."

The fact that she had so carefully cherished the contract I signed must have doomed Grimm.

...At that moment, I notice something around Grimm's neck.

It's the necklace I tried to take back after finding out it was a marriage proposal.

Oh, right. I remember being turned off by how happy she was when I gave it to her...

I guess I'll bury her with it.

After making that decision, I reach over, removing the necklace when—

The necklace vanishes in a flash of light.

"...That's not my fault, right? I didn't do anything bad."

I reflexively make my excuses, but obviously there's no one here to respond.

As if triggered by that one event, the other sentimental items around me start vanishing in bursts of light.

Oh, hey, this is...

"Hey, Grimm, I see you're finally up."

"...This is the second time. The second time I've woken up to see you next to me, Commander..."

That's right. I sat here waiting the first time we resurrected Grimm after meeting her.

"Should we go on a date next?"

Grimm smiles happily at my quip.

"I'll pass. For some reason, I was dreaming about getting yelled at by some weird hysterical woman… She kept asking me how many times I intended to repeat the same mistake, and that while it was fortunate the festival went smoothly, I need to get my act together…"

"I'm pretty sure that's the actual Zenarith. She's angry that you keep killing yourself in spite of being undead."

I guess my words are particularly funny to Grimm, because she seems to be holding back a fit of laughter.

"Heh, don't be silly. Undead don't kill themselves. You always say the oddest things, Commander… I guess I lost conscious when I spent so much of my energy on cleansing Gadalkand. But still, you didn't need to bring me here. It's not like I was dead or anything."

"I hate to break it to you, but you were. Things were so bad, it took a pile of offerings to get you up again."

Grimm can no longer hold back her laughter and breaks into a giggle fit.

"All right, all right. If you say so. Tsk, tsk, Commander, always joking…… Huh?"

Not believing a word I say, Grimm suddenly presses her hand to her collar.

"Huh? W-wait, what's going on? It's gone! *Gone!*"

"Nah, you've got plenty. It's just that Snow's are huge."

"Shush! I'm not talking about that! I mean, sure, I've got plenty, but… Never mind that! The necklace you gave me is gone, Commander!"

Grimm searches frantically, tears welling up in her eyes.

"Oh, that? Yeah, it vanished when you came back to life."

"No waaaaaay! So wait, I was actually dead?!"

That's what I've been saying the whole time.

"W-wait, you mean…? I actually removed my own blessing?! Right after showing off like that?"

"Yup. After making a big show of it, you killed yourself."

"Nooooooooooooo!" Grimm suddenly breaks down in tears. "The Undead Festival was a disaster with all those things going wrong, but to top it all off with such an embarrassing display…! Ohhh, Lord Zenarith, the necklace! Please give me back my necklace!"

"H-hold on! That's the god you worship! You'll get punished and die again!"

I hurriedly stop Grimm as she starts hitting the little altar dedicated to Zenarith.

"B-but—but—but it was the engagement necklace you gave me…!"

"I'll buy you something else, okay? Oh, and just for the record, in my country, we have engagement rings instead."

Grimm looks up at me tearfully. "Th-then a ring…"

"Earrings, okay?"

Grimm grabs hold of my arm and begins to throw a tantrum despite her age.

"F-fine, okay… Soon, all right? Soon. But hey, since the necklace is gone, the promise about getting married a decade from now is null and void, okay?"

"Excuuuuuse me?! What are you on about? Are you looking to be cursed? I've got a signed contract here; I'll take you to court! …H-huh? It's gone! The contract is gone!"

Oh, right…

"The contract vanished with your necklace. The necklace and contract must've been really important to you, huh?"

"Noooooooooooooo!"

A good while later…

"Hey, Six. Grimm's finally up, eh?"

After agreeing to the marriage contract a second time and finally getting Grimm to stop crying, I run into Alice and the rest of the Kisaragi Combat Agents.

"Alice, and the Commander's... Huh, where's Snow and Rose?" Grimm asks.

"Snow's locked up in the dungeon for various reasons," Alice replies. "She's probably getting what's coming to her right now. As for Rose... She started saying she wants to stay at a particular old man's house as his pet."

"Sorry—wait. I can't understand any of this. Can you give me the long version?"

When commanding the knights, Snow, in her rush to secure glory for herself, abandoned any pretense of maintaining order. She's currently stewing in the dungeon after Tillis tossed her there.

Since it was Snow's lack of communication that led to the scuffles with Tiger Man, her already-meager salary's been docked again.

As for Rose, it looks like she's gotten used to her life of eating and lying around at that geezer's house and plans to live her life as Patrasche from now on.

"Forget about them for now. They'll be back eventually. We need to focus on this damned forest."

With that, Alice heads out to fetch a particular piece of equipment.

It's now a little bit before dusk.

We're about to throw the full weight of Kisaragi into finishing our fortress.

"Wh-what is it? What are we starting?"

"We're going to build our hideout. Before, we were letting the planet's critters have their way with us, but now we're going to show them the full extent of our power."

We were planning to start construction at dawn, so it's convenient Grimm woke up before that.

It's a good chance to show off our power.

As Grimm stares blankly, one of the agents calls out while avoiding directly entering the forest.

*   *   *

"Activate the Destroyer!"

With that, the heavy rumble of an engine echoes through the air.

Kisaragi's giant multi-legged combat vehicle: the Destroyer.

A mainstay weapon developed by Lilith to fight the giant robots favored by Heroes.

Alice had been patiently repairing it since it'd suffered damage to its various pieces last time, but it's finally operational and ready to go.

With it by our side, we have nothing to fear. Not zombies, not mokemokes.

Even pretty women that grow out of the forest can't pierce the Destroyer's armor.

"Target: the Cursed Forest. All right, you bastards! Time to ravage this world!" Alice calls out from the cockpit of the Destroyer.

The other agents let out a loud cheer, and so begins our settlement of the forest and construction of our hideout—

"...Sometimes you really impress me..."

Grimm sounds exasperated.

"Of course I do," I reply, gazing up at the hideout. "I'm your commander, after all. Why wouldn't you be?"

"But you didn't do anything... Still, you've always impressed me, Commander."

I smirk at Grimm's teasing. "Remember this moment, Grimm. This is where our legend begins. This will be our base: the Grace Kingdom Front Fortress!"

The cheers of the assembled Combat Agents echo all around us.

As the light of dawn illuminates our brand-new fortress, it seems to respond to our cheers and then...

...the whole thing explodes spectacularly.

[Orders to Deployed Combatants]

After the Heroes staged their massive counterassault on Earth and both sides suffered heavy losses, we are currently locked in stalemate.

To overcome this impasse, we will be sending a Supreme Leader to the planet where Agent Six is dispatched to swiftly place it under our control.

Once secured, we will recall the deployed assets and concentrate our forces against the Heroes.

According to our current reports, the local competition's forces will not pose a threat to a Supreme Leader.

We hereby order the completion of the fortress to house a Supreme Leader.

We place our faith in the plan proposed by Alice to utilize the Destroyer to settle the Cursed Forest and complete the fortress.

The Supreme Leader to be deployed will be communicated at a later date. There will be no need for regular reports from here onward.

Issued by Astaroth

P.S. We require a precise explanation on the item in the last report detailing that Agent 6 has pledged his future to a particular partner (hereafter removed).

AFTERWORD

Thank you for picking up Volume 3 of *Combatants Will Be Dispatched!*

It's been a while since Volume 2 was released, but I've finally been able to complete Volume 3.

My sincerest apologies to all the readers who were patiently waiting for Volume 3.

I'll say here that I'll do my best to get the next book out more quickly, but please take it more as a statement of intent than a firm promise.

This volume features Grimm, who's usually either sleeping or chasing after men.

Of course, this isn't a series focusing on exploring what makes each heroine unique and attractive, so please don't read too much into it when a volume's presented as "XX's volume."

The story line uses the Obon Festival as a motif, and it turns out that of all the squad members, Grimm's actually supposed to be the most sensible one.

Snow, loyal to money due to her rough upbringing, has no qualms about using her body.

Rose is willing to eat even the main character if the situation calls for it.

Alice is the evil android who worships at the altar of science and is the quintessential cynic.

With a lineup like that, I think that Grimm—who is faithful to the person she falls in love with, is skilled at most domestic tasks, and even has a nest egg saved up for marriage—actually ends up having the highest heroine score.

Of course, this series won't end up as a romcom, so those traits are actually meaningless...

This is a pretty pointless bit of trivia, but in the author's series *Konosuba: God's Blessing on This Wonderful World!* a deity named Regina, the Goddess of Manipulation and Revenge, makes an appearance.

This character is actually a sister to Zenarith, the Goddess of Undeath and Disaster, from this series. However, since the two sisters handle different worlds, I doubt this fact will have any bearing in either work.

There might be stories that have hints like that scattered in the world building. In that case, I'll probably make note of it in the afterword.

So for this volume, I'd like to once again close by thanking the illustrator Kakao Lanthanum, my editor I——, and everyone else in the editorial department for helping me get this book out the door.

And of course, as has become the habit—

—heartfelt thanks to all the readers who picked up this volume!

Natsume Akatsuki